ESSENTIAL GERMAN

Nicole Irving & Leslie Colvin
Illustrated by Ann Johns
Designed by Adrienne Kern

Additional designs by Brian Robertson

Language consultants: Anke Kornmüller
& Gene O. Stimpson
Series editor: Gaby Waters

Contents

About this book

This phrase book will help you to survive, travel and socialize. It supplies simple, up-to-date German for holidays and exchange visits. It also gives basic information about Germany and tips for low budget travellers.

The language is everyday, spoken German. This can differ from textbook German and ranges from the correct to the colloquial, and from the polite to the casual, depending on the region, the situation and the person speaking.

Use the Contents list to find the section you need or look up words in the Index. Always remember that you can make yourself clear with words that are not quite right or with very few words. Saying *"Hamburg?"* while pointing at a train will provoke *ja* or *nein* (yes or no). Words like *bitte* (excuse me) or *danke* (thank you) make anything sound more polite and generally guarantee a

friendly response. For anyone who is ready to have a go, the German listed below is absolutely essential.

● Newcomers to German should look through German pronunciation and How German works (pages 50-53).

● Words are given in the form likely to be most useful. The level of politeness is pitched to suit each situation and casual *du* or polite *Sie* forms are given as appropriate. Sometimes you will have to judge which is best so both are given. If in doubt, say *Sie*.

● The German letter *ß* is like "ss".

● An asterisk after a German word shows it is slang or fairly familiar, e.g. depressed *down**.

● (m) is short for masculine, (f) for feminine and (n) for neuter.

Absolute essentials

Do you speak English?	*Sprechen Sie Englisch?*[1]	1 *eins*	11 *elf*
	Sprichst du Englisch?[2]	2 *zwei*	12 *zwölf*
I don't understand.	*Ich verstehe das nicht.*	3 *drei*	13 *dreizehn*
Can you write it down?	*Können Sie das aufschreiben?*[1]	4 *vier*	14 *vierzehn*
	Kannst du das aufschreiben?[2]	5 *fünf*	15 *fünfzehn*
Can you say that again?	*Können Sie das noch einmal sagen?*[1]	6 *sechs*	16 *sechzehn*
	Kannst du das noch einmal sagen?[2]	7 *sieben*	17 *siebzehn*
A bit slower, please.	*Etwas langsamer, bitte.*	8 *acht*	18 *achtzehn*
What does this word mean?	*Was bedeutet dieses Wort?*	9 *neun*	19 *neunzehn*
What's the German for this?	*Wie heißt das auf Deutsch?*	10 *zehn*	20 *zwanzig*

yes	*ja*	hello	*hallo*	why?	*warum?*
no	*nein*	goodbye	*auf*	because	*weil*
maybe	*vielleicht*		*Wiedersehen*	how?	*wie?*
I don't know.	*Ich weiß nicht.*	hi	*hi, hallo*	how much?	*wieviel?*
I don't mind.	*Das ist mir*	bye	*tschüs*	how many?	*wieviele?*
	egal.			How much is it?	*Was kostet*
		good morning	*guten Morgen*		*das?*
please	*bitte*	good evening	*guten Abend*		
thank you	*danke*	good night	*gute Nacht*	What is it/this?	*Was ist das?*
sorry	*Entschuldigung*			it/this is	*das ist*
excuse me	*entschuldigen*	and	*und*	is there?	*gibt es?*
	Sie[1]	or	*oder*	there is	*es gibt*
	entschuldige[2]				
I'm (very)	*es tut mir*	when?	*wann?*	I'd like	*ich möchte*
sorry	*(sehr) leid*	where?	*wo?*	could I have?	*ich hätte gern*

Fact file

You will find a *Fremdenverkehrsbüro* (tourist office), sometimes called *Verkehrsverein*, in most big towns and cities. It's often near the station or town hall. In tourist areas even small towns have one but opening times may be restricted.

Most tourist offices provide town plans and leaflets on local sights free of charge. They also give advice on places to stay and travel arrangements. They often employ someone who speaks English. Some tourist offices sell maps and specialist booklets on local footpaths, wildlife etc. Some of these may be available in English.

Directions

It's on the left/right.	*Es ist auf der linken/ rechten Seite.*
Turn left/right.	*Biegen Sie nach links/rechts ab.*
Go straight ahead.	*Gehen Sie geradeaus.*
Take...	*Nehmen Sie...*
the first on the left	*die erste Straße links*
the second on the right	*die zweite Straße rechts*
the third	*die dritte*
the fourth	*die vierte*
Follow the signs...	*Folgen Sie dem Schild...*
for Bonn	*nach Bonn*
for the station	*zum Bahnhof*
It's...	*Es ist...*
Go...	*Gehen Sie...*
Turn...	*Biegen Sie ab nach...*
left	*links*
right	*rechts*
straight ahead	*geradeaus*
on the left	*auf der linken Seite*
on the right	*auf der rechten Seite*
crossroads, junction	*Kreuzung*
roundabout	*Kreisverkehr*
traffic lights	*Ampel*
pedestrian crossing	*Fußgängerüberweg*
zebra crossing	*Zebrastreifen*
subway	*Unterführung*
Cross...	*Überqueren Sie...*
Follow...	*Folgen Sie...*
street, road	*die Straße*
alley	*der Weg, die Gasse*
path, footpath	*der Fußweg*
cycle path	*der Fahrradweg*
main/high street	*die Hauptstraße*

square	der Platz
dual carriageway	die Schnellstraße
motorway	die Autobahn
ringroad	Umgehungsstraße
one way	Einbahnstraße
no entry	keine Einfahrt
dead end	Sackgasse
no parking	Parken verboten
car park	der Parkplatz
parking meters	Parkuhren
pedestrian area	die Fußgängerzone
pedestrians	Fußgänger
pavement	der Bürgersteig
town centre	die Stadtmitte, das Zentrum, die City[1]
area, part of town	das Stadtviertel, der Stadtteil
suburb	der Vorort
outskirts, suburbs	der Stadtrand
town hall	das Rathaus
bridge	die Brücke
river	der Fluß
railway line	die Eisenbahnlinie
post office	die Post, das Postamt
shops	die Geschäfte
church	die Kirche
school	die Schule
cinema	das Kino
museum	das Museum
park	der Park
just before the	kurz vor
just after the	kurz nach
at the end	am Ende
on the corner	an der Ecke
next to	neben
opposite	gegenüber
in front of	vor
behind	hinter
over	über
under	unter
in	in
on	auf
here	hier
there	dort
over there	da drüben
far	weit
near, nearby	in der Nähe
near here, around here	hier in der Nähe
in this area	in der Gegend
somewhere	irgendwo
10 minutes walk	zehn Minuten zu Fuß
5 minutes drive	fünf Minuten im Auto
by bike	mit dem Rad
on foot	zu Fuß

Wie kommt man am besten zum Campingplatz?
What's the best way to the campsite?

Können Sie mir das auf dem Plan zeigen?
Can you show me on the map?

Wo ist der nächste Strand?
Where's the nearest beach?

Wie weit ist das?
How far is it?

Wie komme ich zur Jugendherberge?
How do I get to the youth hostel?

---

[1] City is often used to mean town centre, e.g. Ich gehe in die City (I'm going to town).

Travel: trains, underground, buses

Getting information

Wann geht der nächste Zug nach Berlin?

Wie lange dauert die Fahrt?

Muß ich umsteigen?

What time is the next train to Berlin?

How long is the journey?

Do I have to change?

Tickets

Wo kann ich eine Fahrkarte kaufen?

Wie funktioniert dieser Automat?

Einmal Mainz einfach, bitte.

Where can I buy a ticket?

How does this machine work?

Can I have a single to Mainz?

Finding the right bus

Ist das der richtige Bus nach Hamburg?

Wohin fährt dieser Bus?

Können Sie mir sagen, wo ich aussteigen muß?

Is this the right bus for Hamburg?

Where does this bus go?

Can you tell me where to get off?

Wo steige ich um, um in die Friedrichstraße zu kommen?

Von welchem Bahnsteig fährt der Zug zum Marienplatz?

Was wurde gerade über Lautsprecher gesagt?

Where do I change for Friedrichstraße?

What did they just say over the loudspeaker?

Which platform do I need for Marienplatz?

Bekomme ich Ermäßigung?

Can I get a reduction?

Fact file

DB (German national railways) runs a good rail network and many bus services. *IC* or *Intercity* are high speed trains for which you pay a supplement. There are various cheap deals, e.g. *DB Tourist Card* for four, nine or 16 days travel and *Saver* or *Super Saver* tickets for cheap, long-distance travel at off-peak times.

The local transport system varies from city to city, but it's usually a combination of bus, tram, underground and *S-Bahn* (suburban rail network). The same tickets are often valid for all types of transport. You may need several tickets for long journeys. There are ticket machines at stations and bus and tram stops; you can sometimes buy tickets from bus or tram drivers. Tickets are sold singly or in blocks which work out cheaper. Most cities also have cheap local travel deals such as a *Tageskarte* (day pass). Normally you have to stamp your ticket in special machines before travelling or as you get on the bus or tram.

railway station	*der Bahnhof*	ticket	*eine Fahrkarte*
underground station	*die U-Bahn-Station*	a single [2]	*einfach*
bus station	*der Busbahnhof*	a return	*hin und zurück*
bus stop	*die Bushaltestelle*	book of tickets	*eine Mehrfahrtenkarte*
train	*der Zug*	supplement	*ein Zuschlag*
underground train	*die U-Bahn*	I'd like to reserve a	*Ich möchte einen*
tram	*die Straßenbahn*	seat.	*Sitzplatz reservieren.*
bus, coach	*der Bus*	left luggage lockers	*Schließfächer*
leaves at 2 [1]	*fährt um zwei Uhr ab*	map	*eine Karte, ein Plan*
arrives at 4.30	*kommt um halb fünf an*	timetable	*ein Fahrplan*
first	*erste*	arrivals	*Ankunft*
last	*letzte*	departures	*Abfahrt, Abflug*
next	*nächste*	long distance train	*Fernzug*
cheapest	*billigste*	local, suburban	*Nahverkehr*
ticket office	*der Fahrkartenschalter*	every day	*täglich*
ticket machine	*der Fahrkartenautomat*	weekdays [1]	*wochentags*
fare	*der Fahrpreis*	Sundays and holidays	*an Sonn- und*
student fare	*Studentenermäßigung*		*Feiertagen*
youth fare	*Fahrpreis für Jugendliche*	except	*außer*

[1]For times, days of the week etc. see page 54. [2]The proper word for a return ticket is *eine Rückfahrkarte*, but most people say *Einmal Mainz hin und zurück* (A return to Mainz).

Travel: air, sea, road

Air and sea

> Kann ich meinen Flug bestätigen?

> Wann muß ich einchecken?

> Wo ist die Abfertigung?

I'd like to confirm my flight.

What time should I check in?

Where do I check in?

> Mein Gepäck ist nicht angekommen.

> Frau Schulz sollte mich abholen.

My luggage hasn't arrived.

Mrs Schulz is supposed to be meeting me.

Fact file

Airports and harbours often have signs and announcements in English. There's usually a bus or train from the airport into town — generally the cheapest option.

Taxis have a standard pick-up charge plus a metered fare; each large bag is charged extra. Taxis often take only three passengers, but can still be good value.

Ich möchte nach...
Take me to...
Was kostet es zur...?
What's the fare to...?
Setzen Sie mich bitte hier ab.
Please drop me here.

airport	der Flughafen	customs	der Zoll
port	der Hafen	visa	ein Visum
aeroplane	das Flugzeug	passport	ein Paß
ferry	die Fähre	departure gate	Ausgang
hovercraft	das Hovercraft	boarding pass	die Bordkarte
flight	der Flug	foot passenger	ein Passagier
(sea) crossing	die Überfahrt	ticket	ein Fahrschein
North Sea	Nordsee	No smoking	Nichtraucher
Baltic Sea	Ostsee		
rough	stürmisch	travel agent	ein Reisebüro
calm	ruhig	special offer	Sonderangebot
I feel sea sick.	Mir ist schlecht.	airline ticket	der Flugschein
on board	an Bord	standby	Standby
suitcase	der Koffer	charter flight	Charterflug
backpack, rucksack	der Rucksack	round the world trip	Weltreise
bag	die Tasche	flight number	die Flugnummer
hand luggage	Handgepäck	a booking	eine Reservierung
heavy	schwer	to change	ändern
trolleys	Gepäckwagen	to cancel	stornieren
information	die Auskunft	a delay	Verspätung

[1]See page 41 for different kinds of bikes.

On the road

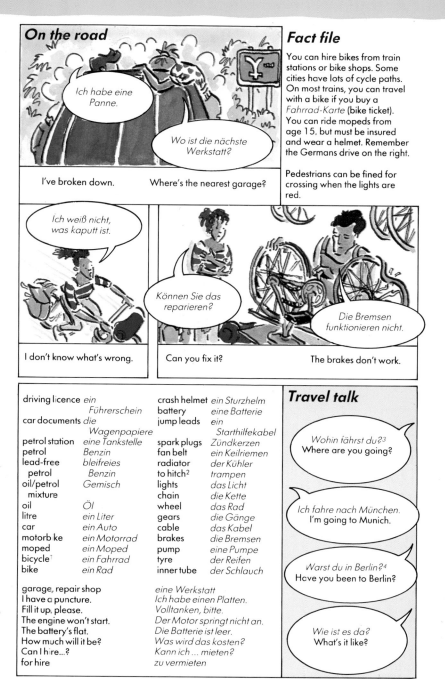

Ich habe eine Panne.

I've broken down.

Wo ist die nächste Werkstatt?

Where's the nearest garage?

Ich weiß nicht, was kaputt ist.

I don't know what's wrong.

Können Sie das reparieren?

Can you fix it?

Die Bremsen funktionieren nicht.

The brakes don't work.

Fact file

You can hire bikes from train stations or bike shops. Some cities have lots of cycle paths. On most trains, you can travel with a bike if you buy a *Fahrrad-Karte* (bike ticket). You can ride mopeds from age 15. but must be insured and wear a helmet. Remember the Germans drive on the right.

Pedestrians can be fined for crossing when the lights are red.

driving licence	*ein Führerschein*	crash helmet	*ein Sturzhelm*
car documents	*die Wagenpapiere*	battery	*eine Batterie*
petrol station	*eine Tankstelle*	jump leads	*ein Starthilfekabel*
petrol	*Benzin*	spark plugs	*Zündkerzen*
lead-free petrol	*bleifreies Benzin*	fan belt	*ein Keilriemen*
oil/petrol mixture	*Gemisch*	radiator	*der Kühler*
oil	*Öl*	to hitch[2]	*trampen*
litre	*ein Liter*	lights	*das Licht*
car	*ein Auto*	chain	*die Kette*
motorbike	*ein Motorrad*	wheel	*das Rad*
moped	*ein Moped*	gears	*die Gänge*
bicycle[1]	*ein Fahrrad*	cable	*das Kabel*
bike	*ein Rad*	brakes	*die Bremsen*
		pump	*eine Pumpe*
		tyre	*der Reifen*
		inner tube	*der Schlauch*

garage, repair shop	*eine Werkstatt*
I have a puncture.	*Ich habe einen Platten.*
Fill it up, please.	*Volltanken, bitte.*
The engine won't start.	*Der Motor springt nicht an.*
The battery's flat.	*Die Batterie ist leer.*
How much will it be?	*Was wird das kosten?*
Can I hire...?	*Kann ich ... mieten?*
for hire	*zu vermieten*

Travel talk

Wohin fährst du?[3]
Where are you going?

Ich fahre nach München.
I'm going to Munich.

Warst du in Berlin?[4]
Have you been to Berlin?

Wie ist es da?
What's it like?

[2]It's not advisable to hitch, but there are *Mitfahrzentralen* (ride sharing organizations), in most large cities. [3]/[4]The polite forms are [3]*Wohin fahren Sie?* [4]*Waren Sie in ..?* See page 51.

9

Accommodation: places to stay

At the Tourist office

Haben Sie ein Campingplatz-Verzeichnis?

Können Sie für mich ein Zimmer reservieren?

Ich möchte ein Zimmer für zwei Personen.

Do you have a list of campsites?

I'm looking for a room for two people.

Can you book a room for me?

Hotels

Haben Sie ein Zimmer?

Wir sind belegt.

Gibt es hier in der Nähe noch ein Hotel?

Do you have a room?

We're full.

Is there another hotel nearby?

Fact file

The *Fremdenverkehrsbüro* or *Verkehrsamt* (tourist office) will supply lists of places to stay and can make bookings for you.

There are lots of *Jugendherbergen* (youth hostels) in Germany, all very good and cheap. You need to be a member of the IYHA[1]. *Campingplätze* (campsites) are generally good and can be cheap. You may pay extra for hot showers.

A *Pension* (guest house) or *Gasthof* (country inn) provides *Fremdenzimmer* (guest rooms), at reasonable rates, but *Hotels* can be pricey. Look out for the sign *Zimmer frei* (rooms to let in private houses).

Camping

Haben Sie noch Platz?

Do you have a space?

[1]International Youth Hostel Association.

Rooms to let	Zimmer frei	Can I have my passport back?	Kann ich meinen Paß zurückhaben?
How much do you want to pay?	Wieviel möchten Sie bezahlen?		
How many nights?	Wie lange bleiben Sie?	tent	ein Zelt
one/two night(s)	eine Nacht/zwei Nächte	caravan	ein Wohnwagen
single room	ein Einzelzimmer	restaurant	ein Restaurant
double room	ein Doppelzimmer	swimming pool	ein Schwimmbad, ein Swimming-pool
room with 3 beds	ein Dreibettzimmer		
clean	sauber	hot water	warmes Wasser
cheap	billig	cold water	kaltes Wasser
expensive	teuer	drinking water	Trinkwasser
lunch	das Mittagessen	camping gas	Campinggas
dinner	das Abendessen	guy rope	eine Zeltschnur
full board	Vollpension	tent rings	die Zeltringe
half board	Halbpension	tent peg	ein Hering
bed and breakfast	Übernachtung mit Frühstück	mallet	ein Holzhammer
		torch	eine Taschenlampe
key	der Schlüssel	matches	Streichhölzer
room number	die Zimmernummer	loo paper	Klopapier
registration form	das Anmeldeformular	can opener	ein Dosenöffner

Was kostet ein Zimmer?

How much for a room?

Ist das mit Frühstück?

Does that include breakfast?

Kann ich das Zimmer sehen?

Can I see the room?

Wir sind zu dritt mit einem Zelt.

Gibt's hier einen Laden?

Kann man das Wasser trinken?

Wo kann man schwimmen gehen?

There are three of us with a tent.

Do you have a shop?

Is it OK to drink the tap water?

Where's the best place to swim?

Greetings

Hallo.
Hello.

Wie geht's?
How are you?

Wo soll ich mein Zeug hin tun?
Where can I put my things?

Wo schlafe ich?
Where am I sleeping?

Wann frühstückt ihr?[1]
What time do you have breakfast?

Kannst du mich um sieben wecken?[2]
Could you wake me up at seven?

For more polite or formal greetings, say *Guten Tag* (good day) followed by *Herr X* or *Frau X* (Mr X or Mrs X). Also use the polite form: *Wie geht es Ihnen?* (How are you?)

Washing

Wie funktioniert die Dusche?
How does your shower work?

Stört es, wenn ich ein paar Sachen wasche?
Do you mind if I wash a few things?

Is it OK to have a bath?	*Ist es okay, wenn ich bade?*	bath	*das Bad*
Can I borrow a towel?	*Kann ich ein Handtuch haben?*	shower	*die Dusche*
		bidet	*das Bidet*
Where can I dry these?	*Wo kann ich das trocknen?*	towel	*ein Handtuch*
		a bar of soap	*ein Stück Seife*
		shampoo	*das Shampoo*
		deodorant	*ein Deo(dorant)*
bathroom	*das Badezimmer*	toothpaste	*Zahnpasta*
toilet	*die Toilette*	hairdryer	*ein Fön*
loo	*das Klo*	washing powder	*Waschpulver*

[1]/[2]/[3]To be polite, when speaking to a stranger or an older person, say [1]*Wann frühstücken Sie?* [2]*Können Sie mich* etc. [3]*Nett von Ihnen, daß* etc. See page 51.

Being polite

Kann ich etwas dazu beisteuern?

Nein, es ist in Ordnung.

Can I pay my share?

No, it's OK.

Nett von euch, daß ich hier wohnen kann.[3]

Wenn ich was brauche, frag' ich.

It's nice of you to let me stay.

I'll ask if I need anything.

Saying goodbye

Vielen Dank. Thank you for everything.

Auf Wiedersehen. Goodbye.

Using the phone

Kann ich das Telefon benutzen?
Can I use your phone?

Ich bezahle das Gespräch.
I'll pay for the call.

Was kostet es, in England anzurufen?
How much is it to call Britain?

See page 15 for more about phones and making phone calls.

I'm tired.	Ich bin müde.
I'm knackered.	Ich bin völlig kaputt.
I'm cold.	Mir ist kalt.
I'm hot.	Mir ist heiß.
I'm fine.	Ich fühle mich wohl.
Can I have a key?	Kann ich einen Schlüssel haben?
What is there to do in the evenings?	Was kann man abends machen?
Where's the nearest phone box?	Wo ist die nächste Telefonzelle?
alarm clock	ein Wecker
sleeping bag	ein Schlafsack
on the floor	auf dem Boden
an extra...	noch ein/eine...
blanket	eine Decke
duvet	eine Bettdecke
sheet	ein Laken
pillow	ein Kopfkissen
electric socket	eine Steckdose
needle and thread	Nadel und Faden
scissors	eine Schere
iron	ein Bügeleisen
upstairs	oben
downstairs	unten
cupboard	ein Schrank
bedroom	das Schlafzimmer
living room	das Wohnzimmer
kitchen	die Küche
garden	der Garten
balcony	der Balkon

Banks, post offices, phones

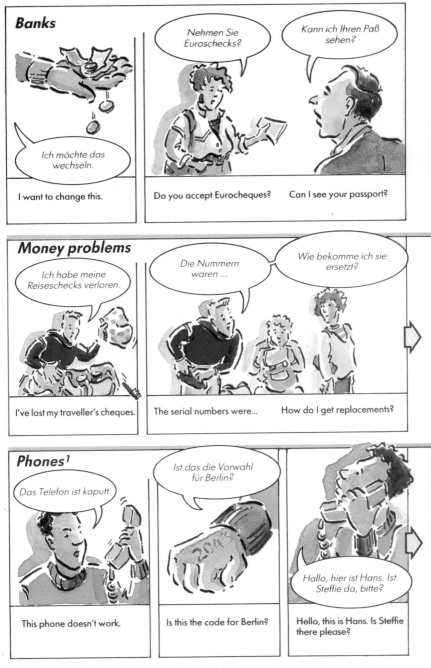

Banks

Ich möchte das wechseln.

I want to change this.

Nehmen Sie Euroschecks?

Do you accept Eurocheques?

Kann ich Ihren Paß sehen?

Can I see your passport?

Money problems

Ich habe meine Reiseschecks verloren.

I've lost my traveller's cheques.

Die Nummern waren ...

The serial numbers were...

Wie bekomme ich sie ersetzt?

How do I get replacements?

Phones[1]

Das Telefon ist kaputt.

This phone doesn't work.

Ist das die Vorwahl für Berlin?

Is this the code for Berlin?

Hallo, hier ist Hans. Ist Steffie da, bitte?

Hello, this is Hans. Is Steffie there please?

[1]For more phrases on using the phone see page 13.

bank	eine Bank	a stamp for	eine Briefmarke für
cashier's desk, till	die Kasse	Britain	England/Groß
foreign exchange	Devisen, Wechsel		Britannien
enquiries	Auskunft, Information	the USA	Amerika
money	Geld	Australia[2]	Australien
small change	Kleingeld	by airmail	per Luftpost
traveller's cheques	Reiseschecks	by registered	per Einschreiben
credit card	eine Kreditkarte	post	
exchange rate	der Wechselkurs	poste restante	postlagernd
commission	die Provision		
a (money) transfer	eine Überweisung	telephone	ein Telefon
from Britain	aus England	telephone box	eine Telefonzelle
		directory	das Telefonbuch
post office	ein Postamt	(phone) number	die (Telefon) nummer
postcard	eine Postkarte	extension (12)	Apparat (zwölf)
letter	ein Brief	wrong number	falsch verbunden
parcel	ein Paket	reverse charge	ein R-Gespräch
envelope	ein Umschlag	call[3]	
writing paper	Schreibpapier	Hang on.	Bleib' am Apparat.

Post offices

Ich erwarte Geld, ist es da?

I'm expecting some money, has it arrived?

Kann ich hierfür eine Briefmarke haben?

Can I have a stamp for this?

Wo ist der nächste Briefkasten?

Where's the nearest postbox?

Wann ist sie zurück?
When will she be back?

Kann ich eine Nachricht hinterlassen für...?
Can I leave a message for...?

Sagen Sie ihr/ihm bitte, daß ich angerufen habe.

Kann sie/er mich zurückrufen?
Can she/he call me back?

Please tell her/him I called.

Meine Nummer ist...
My number is...

Fact file

The unit of currency is the *Deutsche Mark* (DM). 1 DM = 100 *Pfennige*. Most banks are open Monday to Friday 8.30-12.30 and 2-4 (6 on Thursday). *Wechselstuben* (foreign exchange offices) are often open outside banking hours but you may get a poorer rate of exchange.

There are pay phones on the street, in post offices, cafés and department stores. Most take coins but some take *Telefonkarten* (phonecards) which you can buy at a post office. You can make international calls from most pay phones. Look for the sign *Ausland*. For useful phone numbers see page 47.

You can get stamps from machines outside post offices and on some post boxes.

[2]For other countries see page 55. [3]Reverse charge calls are not possible within Germany, but can be made to some other countries.

Cafés

café	*ein Café*
pub, bar	*eine Kneipe*
table	*ein Tisch*
chair	*ein Stuhl*
Cheers!	*Prost!*
something to drink	*etwas zu trinken*
something to eat	*etwas zu essen*
coffee[1]	*ein Kaffee*
lemon tea	*ein Tee mit Zitrone*
tea with milk	*ein Tee mit Milch*
hot chocolate	*eine heiße Schokolade*
fruit juice	*ein Fruchtsaft*
apple juice	*ein Apfelsaft*
coke	*eine Cola*
mineral water	*ein Mineralwasser*
still	*ohne Kohlensäure*
fizzy	*mit Kohlensäure*
bottle of beer	*eine Flasche Bier*
draught beer	*ein Bier vom Faß*
glass of red wine	*ein Glas Rotwein*
half bottle of white wine	*eine halbe Flasche Weißwein*
milk	*Milch*
cream	*Sahne*
sugar	*Zucker*
with ice	*mit Eis*
slice of lemon	*eine Scheibe Zitrone*
with	*mit*
without	*ohne*
omelette	*ein Omelett*
cheese sandwich	*ein Käsebrot*
ham sandwich	*ein Schinkenbrot*
ice-cream	*ein Eis*

Fact file

Cafés are open during the day for drinks, snacks, meeting friends or using the loo and phone. Other options: Italian ice-cream places (names like *Eis-Napoli* or *Eis-Milano*), *Café-Konditorei* (for coffee and cakes), *Gaststätte* (food at mealtimes, soft drinks or beer all day) and *Weinstube* (wine etc. in the evening). Prices are often displayed outside (smart means pricey).

Drinks: try *Apfelschorle* or *Weinschorle* (apple juice or wine with soda).

Snacks: they include *Käsetoast* (toasted cheese sandwich), *belegtes Brot* (sandwich[2]), *Kaffee und Kuchen* (coffee and cakes) which are traditional in the afternoon, or *Torten* (gâteaux).

Wie wär's mit einem Kaffee?
How about a cup of coffee?

Ist hier noch frei?
Is this chair free?

Die Karte, bitte.
Can I see the menu?

Einen Kaffee, bitte.
A coffee, please.

Haben Sie Milchshakes?
Do you have milkshakes?

16 [1] Coffee is usually served black with a jug of milk. [2] This is an open sandwich which is the usual way of serving sandwiches.

Eating out[1]

Choosing a place

Wo gehen wir hin?

Ich mag keine Pizza.

Laßt uns einen Kebab essen gehen.

Where shall we go?	I don't like pizzas.	Let's go for a kebab.

German food	*deutsches Essen*	vegetables	*Gemüse*
Italian ...	*italienisches ...*	cheese	*Käse*
Greek ...	*griechisches ...*	fruit	*Obst*
Yugoslav ...	*jugoslawisches ...*	chips[2]	*Fritten*
cheap restaurant	*ein billiges Restaurant*	mashed potato	*Kartoffelbrei*
snack	*ein Imbiß*	salad	*ein Salat*
take-away	*zum Mitnehmen*	spaghetti	*Spaghetti*
menu	*die Karte*	sausage	*ein Würstchen*
starter	*eine Vorspeise*	steak	*ein Steak*
main course	*ein Hauptgericht*	hamburger	*ein Hamburger*
dessert	*eine Nachspeise, ein Nachtisch*	mustard	*Senf*
		salt	*Salz*
		pepper	*Pfeffer*
price	*der Preis*	dressing	*die Salatsoße*
all inclusive	*Inklusivpreise*	mayonnaise	*die Mayonnaise*
fish	*Fisch*	Did you enjoy it?	*Hat es geschmeckt?*
meat	*Fleisch*	Yes, it's very good.	*Ja, gut, danke.*

Problems

Das ist nicht durch.

Ich habe Schnitzel bestellt.

Haben Sie kein Tomatenketchup?

I ordered *Schnitzel*.	This isn't cooked enough.	Don't you have any ketchup?

[1]There are also food words on pages 16, 21 and 25. [2]Chips are often called *Pommes frites* on menus.

Deciding what to have

Was ist das?

What's that?

Ich nehme so einen.

I'll have one of those.

Kann ich einen ohne Käse haben?

Can I have one without cheese?

Fact file

German food varies from region to region and is worth exploring. Specialities you find everywhere include *Schnitzel* (pork or veal, often in breadcrumbs), many kinds of *Würstchen* (sausages), *Frikadelle* (meatballs), *Knödel* (dumplings), *Rotkohl* (red cabbage), *eingelegte Heringe* or *Rollmöpse* (pickled herrings) and many kinds of bread and cakes (see pages 16 and 25).

There are lots of restaurants but many are pricey. *Gaststätte* specialize in serving local food. Look out for the *Tagesmenü* (set menu) which is displayed outside with its price. It is usually three courses and is often good value.

Cheap places to eat are department store cafeterias, hamburger places and *Imbißbuden* (snackbars, many of them Turkish). *Frittenbuden* (food stalls) serve sausages, chips, pizzas, etc. Some foreign restaurants are good value. Try Italian, Greek and Yugoslav.

The bill always includes service and VAT but tipping is normal practice so it's best to leave a small tip.

Best times for eating out are lunch at 12 or 1 and dinner at about 7.30.

It's often cheaper to buy your own food (see page 25).

Hallo!

Excuse me!

Zahlen, bitte!

Can we have the bill please?

Das habe ich nicht bestellt.

I didn't order this.

Eating in

Das Essen ist fertig!
It's ready.
Greift zu!
Help yourselves.
Kann ich die Butter haben?
Can you pass the butter?
Was ist da drin?
What's in this?
Möchtest du Salat?[1]
Would you like some salad?
Ein wenig.
Just a little.
Noch etwas Brot?
Some more bread?

Helping

Kann ich helfen?
Kann ich den Tisch decken?
Kann ich abwaschen?

Can I help?

Can I lay the table?

Can I do the washing-up?

[1]The polite form is *Möchten Sie . . . ?* See page 51.

Ich bin satt, danke.
I've had enough thanks.

Es war köstlich.
That was delicious.

meal	das Essen	pasta	Nudeln
breakfast	das Frühstück	potatoes	Kartoffeln
lunch	das Mittagessen	onions	Zwiebeln
dinner	das Abendessen	garlic	Knoblauch
(evening)		tomatoes	Tomaten
glass	ein Glas	cabbage	Kohl/Kraut
plate	ein Teller	cauliflower	Blumenkohl
knife	ein Messer	beans	Bohnen
fork	eine Gabel	peas	Erbsen
spoon	ein Löffel	carrots	Karotten
bread	Brot	spinach	Spinat
roll	Brötchen	pickled	
boiled egg	gekochtes Ei	cucumber	Gewürzgurke
jam	Konfitüre	cucumber	Salatgurke
margarine	Margarine	pepper (red,	Paprika
		green)	(rot, grün)
chicken	Hähnchen	celery	Stangensellerie
pork	Schweine-	radish	Radieschen
	fleisch	beetroot	Rote Beete
beef	Rindfleisch	artichokes	Artischocken
veal	Kalbfleisch		
liver	Leber	raw	roh
		(too) hot, spicy	(zu) scharf
dumplings	Knödel	salty	salzig
rice	Reis	sweet	süß

Enjoy your meal.   Guter Appetit!
I'm thirsty.   Ich habe Durst.
I'm not hungry.   Ich habe keinen Hunger.

Fact file

Standard breakfast is coffee or tea with rolls or toast and butter and jam. Eggs, cheese or ham are sometimes served.

The main meal is lunch and is often hot. The evening meal is usually cold. People eat *Wurst* (various cold meats, e.g. salami, *Leberwurst*, or liver sausage), different kinds of *Schinken* (ham) and *Käse* (cheese) with bread and salads.

Special cases

Ich mag keinen Fisch.

I don't like fish.

Ich bin Vegetarier.[2]

I'm a vegetarian.

Ich bin allergisch gegen Eier.

I'm allergic to eggs.

[2]If you're a girl say *Vegetarierin*.

Shopping

Kann ich Ihnen helfen?

Ich möchte das da.

Can I help you?

I'd like one of those.

Was kostet das?

Fünfundzwanzig Mark.

How much is that?

25 marks.

Das ist okay.

Können Sie das bitte aufschreiben?

Ich nehme das.

Please write that down.

That's OK.   I'll take it.

Shops

shop	ein Laden, ein Geschäft
department store	ein Kaufhaus
supermarket	ein Supermarkt
market	der Markt
baker	eine Bäckerei
cake shop	eine Konditorei
grocer	ein Lebens- mittelgeschäft
delicatessen	ein Delikateß- geschäft
butcher	eine Metzgerei, eine Schlachterei
greengrocer	ein Obst- und Gemüse- händler
fishmonger	eine Fisch- handlung
health food shop	ein Reform- haus
household goods shop	ein Haushalts- warengeschäft
dispensing chemist	eine Apotheke
non- dispensing chemist	eine Drogerie, ein Drogerie- markt
jeweller	ein Juwelier
gift shop	ein Geschenk- artikelgeschäft
news kiosk	ein Zeitungskiosk
newsagent	ein Zeitungs- händler
stationer	ein Schreib- warenladen
bookshop	ein Buchladen
record shop	ein Schall- plattenladen
flea market	ein Flohmarkt
sports shop	ein Sport- artikelgeschäft
camping department	die Camping- abteilung
shoe shop	ein Schuh- geschäft
hairdresser, barber	ein Friseur
launderette[1]	ein Waschsalon
dry-cleaner	eine Reinigung
travel agent	ein Reisebüro
open	geöffnet
closed	geschlossen
entrance	der Eingang
exit	der Ausgang
check-out	die Kasse
stairs	die Treppe
price	der Preis

[1]There are very few launderettes. Many campsites and youth hostels have coin operated washing machines.

Fact file

Opening times vary but most shops open Monday to Friday from 8.30 to 6.30. Food shops often open earlier and close at 6 and many small shops close on Wednesday afternoon. On Saturday all shops are open until 1 or 2. On the first Saturday of each month, shops in main shopping areas stay open until 6.

Some news kiosks sell books of bus/tram tickets as well as papers and postcards. An *Apotheke* sells mostly medicines. For everyday things like soap, make-up etc., the cheapest places are a *Drogeriemarkt*, supermarket or department store. Department stores are often the cheapest place for most things. There are lots of them, often in a *Fußgängerzone* (pedestrian area).

Some names to look out for are *Hertie, Karstadt* and *Kaufhof*. The *Abteilung für Haushaltsartikel* (household goods department) sells handy things for camping but for camping equipment, you will need a camping department or sports shop.

For food shopping, most department stores have a self-service *Lebensmittel* (food) hall. Along with supermarkets, these are the easiest and cheapest options. Specialist shops may offer better quality and choice. Bakers do a fantastic range of breads and rolls and are well worth a visit. Markets are held regularly. They are colourful and lively as well as being good for food, local produce and sweets. There are few greengrocers. People buy fruit and vegetables from markets or supermarkets.

Finding the right place

Wo ist das Haupteinkaufsviertel?

Where's the main shopping area?

Haben Sie Batterien?

Do you sell batteries?

Wo bekomme ich welche?

Where can I get some?

Wo kann ich das reparieren lassen?

Where can I get this repaired?

Wo kauft man am besten eine Sonnenbrille?

Where's a good place for sunglasses?

23

I need some sun-tan lotion.

Is there a bigger one?

sunscreen[1]	Sonnenschutzmittel	envelope	ein Umschlag
make-up	Make-up	notepad	ein Notizblock
hair gel	Gel, Haargel	pen	ein Stift
tampons	Tampons	poster	ein Poster
tissues	Papiertaschentücher	stickers	Aufkleber
razor	eine Rasierklinge	badges	Buttons
shaving foam	Rasierschaum	jewellery	Schmuck
aspirin	Aspirin	watch	eine Uhr
plasters	Pflaster	earrings	Ohrringe
contact lens solution	Kontaktlinsenflüssigkeit	ring	ein Ring
		purse	ein Portemonnaie
film	ein Film	bag	eine Tüte
English newspapers	englische Zeitungen	smaller	kleiner
postcard	eine Postkarte	cheaper	billiger
writing paper	Schreibpapier	another colour	eine andere Farbe

Can I help you?   I'm just looking.   Can I see that?

How much is it?   I'll think about it.

Food shopping[2]

Ich möchte zwei Brötchen.

I'd like two rolls.

Kann ich für drei Mark Weintrauben haben?

Can I have 3 marks worth of grapes?

Kann ich ein Stück von dieser Leberwurst haben?

Can I have a bit of that liver sausage?

Soviel?

Like that?

Etwas mehr, bitte.

A bit more please.

Das ist genug, danke.

Ok, that's enough thanks.

carrier-bag	*eine Tragetasche*	cake	*Kuchen*
small	*klein*	pastry	*Stückchen, Teilchen*
big	*groß*	jam doughnut	*Berliner*
a slice of	*eine Scheibe*	sweets	*Süßigkeiten*
a bit more	*etwas mehr*	chocolate	*Schokolade*
a bit less	*etwas weniger*	peanuts	*Erdnüsse*
a portion	*eine Portion*	yoghurt	*ein Joghurt*
a piece of	*ein Stück*	fruit	*Obst*
a kilogram	*ein Kilo*	bananas	*Bananen*
half a kilogram	*ein Pfund*	apples	*Äpfel*
100 grammes	*hundert Gramm*	pears	*Birnen*
health food	*Reformkost, Naturkost*	oranges	*Orangen*
organic	*aus biologischem Anbau*	mandarins	*Mandarinen*
		peaches	*Pfirsiche*
		nectarines	*Nektarinen*
roast chicken	*ein Brathähnchen*	plums	*Pflaumen*
half a chicken	*ein halbes Hähnchen*	apricots	*Aprikosen*
bread	*Brot*	strawberries	*Erdbeeren*
white bread	*Weißbrot*	raspberries	*Himbeeren*
brown bread	*Graubrot*	pineapple	*eine Ananas*
rye bread	*Roggenbrot*	melon	*eine Melone*

[2]See pages 16-21 for more food words.

Clothes

Can I try this on?   Do you have it in a small?   I need a bigger size.

That looks awful.   Does this look OK?   It looks fine.   It doesn't suit me.

The zip's broken.   I've just split my jeans.   Where did you get those?

clothes	Kleider	bra	ein BH[2]
shirt	ein Hemd	tights	eine Strumpfhose
T-shirt	ein T-Shirt		
vest top	ein T-Shirt, ein Top	socks	Socken
sweatshirt	ein Sweatshirt	swimsuit	ein Badeanzug
jumper	ein Pulli	trunks	eine Badehose
cardigan	eine Strickjacke	small	klein
dress	ein Kleid	medium	medium
skirt	ein Rock	large	groß
miniskirt	ein Minirock	too big	zu groß
leggings	Leggings	smaller	kleiner
trousers	Hosen	long	lang
dungarees	Latzhosen	short	kurz
shorts	Shorts	tight	eng
tracksuit	ein Jogginganzug	baggy	(zu) weit
		bright	hell
top	Oberteil	pastel	pastell(farben)
bottom	Hose	fashion	die Mode
trainers	Turnschuhe	look	der Look
shoes	Schuhe	style	der Stil
sandals	Sandalen	fashionable	modisch, in
boots	Stiefel	cool	cool
cowboy boots	Cowboystiefel	trendy	flott, in
		second-hand	gebraucht
braces	Hosenträger	out-of-date	altmodisch
belt	ein Gürtel	smart	schick
coat	ein Mantel	dressy	aufgedonnert
bomber jacket	ein Blouson	scruffy	verlottert
underwear	Unterwäsche	fantastic	super, stark
boxer shorts	Boxershorts	sale	Ausverkauf
pants	eine Unterhose	changing room	die Umkleidekabine

[1]See page 54 for a list of colours. [2]The alphabet and how to pronounce it in German is given on page 50.

27

Music

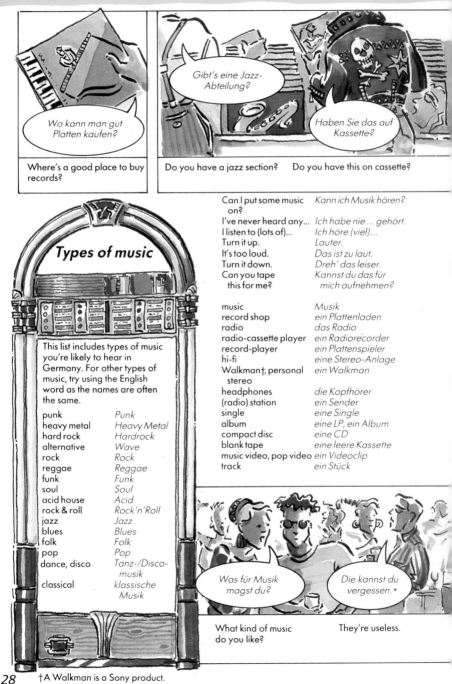

Wo kann man gut Platten kaufen?

Where's a good place to buy records?

Gibt's eine Jazz-Abteilung?

Haben Sie das auf Kassette?

Do you have a jazz section?   Do you have this on cassette?

Types of music

This list includes types of music you're likely to hear in Germany. For other types of music, try using the English word as the names are often the same.

punk	Punk
heavy metal	Heavy Metal
hard rock	Hardrock
alternative	Wave
rock	Rock
reggae	Reggae
funk	Funk
soul	Soul
acid house	Acid
rock & roll	Rock 'n' Roll
jazz	Jazz
blues	Blues
folk	Folk
pop	Pop
dance, disco	Tanz-/Disco-musik
classical	klassische Musik

Can I put some music on?	Kann ich Musik hören?
I've never heard any...	Ich habe nie ... gehört.
I listen to (lots of)...	Ich höre (viel)...
Turn it up.	Lauter.
It's too loud.	Das ist zu laut.
Turn it down.	Dreh' das leiser.
Can you tape this for me?	Kannst du das für mich aufnehmen?
music	Musik
record shop	ein Plattenladen
radio	das Radio
radio-cassette player	ein Radiorecorder
record-player	ein Plattenspieler
hi-fi	eine Stereo-Anlage
Walkman†, personal stereo	ein Walkman
headphones	die Kopfhörer
(radio) station	ein Sender
single	eine Single
album	eine LP, ein Album
compact disc	eine CD
blank tape	eine leere Kassette
music video, pop video	ein Videoclip
track	ein Stück

Was für Musik magst du?

Die kannst du vergessen.*

What kind of music do you like?

They're useless.

†A Walkman is a Sony product.

Von wem ist das?

Kennst du das Video?

Leihst du mir mal diese LP?

| Who's this by? | Have you seen the video? | Can I borrow this album? |

song	ein Song
lyrics	der Text
tune, melody	eine Melodie
rhythm	der Rhythmus
live music	live Musik
group, band	eine Gruppe, eine Band
solo artist	ein Solist
singer	ein Sänger (m), eine Sängerin (f)
accompaniment, backup	die Begleitmusik
member of the group	ein Bandmitglied
fan	ein Fan
tour	eine Tour
concert	ein Konzert
gig	ein Gig, ein Auftritt
charts	die Hitparade, Charts
the Top 10	die Top Ten
number one	die Nummer eins
hit	ein Hit
latest	neuste
new	neu
50's music	Fünfziger Sound

Playing an instrument

Do you play an instrument?	Spielst du ein Instrument?
I play the guitar.	Ich spiele Gitarre.
I'm learning the drums.	Ich lerne Schlagzeug.
I play in a band.	Ich spiele in einer Band.
I sing in a band.	Ich singe in einer Gruppe.
instrument	ein Instrument
piano	Klavier
keyboards	Tastatur, Keyboard
drum machine	Rythmusmaschine
electric guitar	elektrische Gitarre
bass guitar	Baß
saxophone	Saxophon
trumpet	Trompete
harmonica	Mundharmonika
violin	Geige
flute	Flöte
choir	ein Chor
orchestra	ein Orchester

Hast du die neuste LP gehört?

Das ist geil.*

| Have you heard the latest album? | It's brilliant. |

29

Going out: making arrangements, sightseeing

Making arrangements

Na, was steht an?*

Hast du 'ne Idee?

What's happening?   Have you got any
                           ideas?

Machen wir heut'
abend was?

Ich kann nicht, hab'
keine Zeit.

Shall we do something   I can't, I'm busy.
tonight?

Do you know a good place to...	Wo kann man gut...
go dancing?	tanzen gehen?
listen to music?	Musik hören?
eat?	essen?
go for a drink?	etwas trinken gehen?
entertainment guide, listing	ein Programm
club, disco	eine Disco
bar, pub	eine Kneipe
party	eine Fete
picnic	ein Picknick
barbecue	ein Barbecue, ein Grillabend
cinema	das Kino
show	eine Show
ballet	das Ballett
opera	die Oper
in town	in der Stadt
at X's place	bei X

on the beach	am Strand
Can I get a ticket in advance?	Gibt es Karten im Vorverkauf?
ticket office	Vorverkaufstelle, Theaterkasse
student discount	Studentenermäßigung
What time does it open/start?[1]	Wann fängt es an?
What time does it finish?	Wann hört es auf?
open	geöffnet
closed	geschlossen, zu
today	heute
tonight	heute abend
tomorrow	morgen
day after tomorrow	übermorgen
in the morning	morgens
in the afternoon	nachmittags
in the evening	abends
this week	diese Woche
next week	nächste Woche

Sightseeing

What is there to see here?	Was gibt es hier zu sehen?
guide book	ein Reiseführer
sightseeing tour	eine Besichtigungstour
tour	eine Tour, Rundfahrt
sights	Sehenswürdigkeiten
region, area	die Umgebung, die Gegend
countryside	die Landschaft
mountains	die Berge
lake	der See
river	der Fluß
museum	ein Museum
art gallery	eine Galerie
exhibition	eine Ausstellung
the old town	die Altstadt

cathedral	der Dom
church	eine Kirche
castle	ein Schloß
fortress	eine Burg
tower	ein Turm
city walls	eine Stadtmauer
ruins	eine Ruine
amusement arcade	eine Spielhalle
theme park	ein Vergnügungspark
festival	ein Festival
fair, funfair	ein Jahrmarkt, eine Kirmes
fireworks	Feuerwerk
interesting	interessant
dull, boring	langweilig
beautiful	schön

[1]See page 54 for days, dates and time.

Deciding what to do

Fact file

If you want to find out what to visit, go to the tourist office (see page 4). Here you will get free maps, town plans and leaflets.

Local papers have a *Tageskalender* (list of events and entertainments), often best on Saturdays. In the street, *Litfaßsäulen* (pillars) carry posters of events and cinema programmes. Cities have *Veranstaltungsanzeiger* (listings magazines). Films are usually dubbed. Student discounts are common.

Films, TV, books etc.

cinema	ein Kino	with subtitles	mit Untertiteln
theatre	ein Theater	dubbed	synchronisiert
library	eine Bücherei	American	amerikanisch
film, movie	ein Film	well known	bekannt
play	ein Stück, ein Schauspiel	award-winning	preisgekrönt
book	ein Buch	block buster	ein Kinohit
magazine	eine Zeitschrift	a classic	ein Filmklassiker
comic	ein Comic	comedy	eine Komödie
novel	ein Roman	thriller, murder mystery	ein Krimi, ein Thriller
poetry	Gedichte	musical	ein Musical
author, playwright	der Autor	horror film	ein Horrorfilm
director	der Regisseur	adventure film	ein Abenteuerfilm
producer	der Produzent	war film	ein Kriegsfilm
cast	die Besetzung	a western	ein Western
actor	der Schauspieler	a fantasy	ein Fantasiefilm
actress	die Schauspielerin	sci-fi film	ein Science-fiction-Film
film buff	ein Kinofan	a tear jerker	ein sentimentaler Film
production	eine Produktion		
performance	eine Vorstellung	suspense	Spannung
plot	die Handlung	sex	Sex
story	die Geschichte	violence	Gewalt
set	das Bühnenbild	political	politisch
special effects	die Special Effects	satirical	satirisch
photography	die Aufnahmen	serious	ernst
TV	das Fernsehen	offbeat	ungewöhnlich
telly	die Glotze*	commercial	kommerziell
cable TV	das Kabelfernsehen	exciting	aufregend, spannend
satellite TV	Satellitenfernsehen	over the top	übertrieben
programme	die Sendung	good	gut
channel	das Programm	OK, not bad	nicht schlecht
news	die Nachrichten	bad	schlecht
documentary	ein Dokumentarfilm	lousy	schrecklich
serial	eine Sendereihe	silly	blöde
soap	eine Serie, Soap	funny, fun	lustig
ads	die Werbung	soppy	schmalzig
in English	auf englisch	sad	traurig
		scary	gruslig

Talking about yourself

Woher kommst du?

Aus England.

Und du?

Where are you from?   I'm English.   What about you?

Ich wohne in der Nähe von York.

Wo wohnst du?

Wie lange bist du schon hier?

Where do you live?   I live near York.   How long have you been here?

Was machst du in Deutschland?

Wie findest du Deutschland?

Wo wohnst du hier?

What are you doing in Germany?   What do you think of Germany?   Where are you staying?

I'm English.[1]	Ich bin aus England.	my/your	mein[2]/dein[2]
My family is from...[1]	Meine Familie kommt aus...	family	die Familie
I've been here for two weeks.	Ich bin seit zwei Wochen hier.	father/mother	der Vater/die Mutter
I'm on an exchange.	Ich bin als Austausch-	husband/wife	der Mann/die Frau
	student hier.	(my) boyfriend	(mein) Freund
I'm on holiday.	Ich bin auf Urlaub.	(your) girlfriend	(deine) Freundin
I'm staying with friends.	Ich wohne bei Freunden.	brother	der Bruder
		sister	die Schwester
I'm studying German.	Ich studiere Deutsch.	brothers and sisters	Geschwister
I'm travelling around.	Ich reise rum.	single	single
I live ...	Ich wohne ...	married	verheiratet
in the country	auf dem Land	My parents are divorced.	Meine Eltern sind geschieden.
in a town	in einer Stadt	My name is ...	Ich heiße...
in a house	in einem Haus	surname	der Nachname
in a flat	in einer Wohnung	nickname	ein Spitzname
I live with...	Ich wohne zusammen mit...	my address	meine Adresse
I don't live with...	Ich wohne nicht mit... zusammen	My birthday is on the...[3]	Mein Geburtstag ist am...

[1]Words for nationalities, countries and religions are on page 55. [2]*Mein* and *dein* change according to the word you use them with. See page 51. [3]For days and dates, see page 54.

Other people

Gossip

Wer ist das?

Was ist aus Petra geworden?

Wir kommen ganz gut miteinander aus.

Kennst du Klaus?

Wie ist sie?

Who's that?	Do you know Klaus?	What's happened to Petra?	What's she like? We get on OK.

friend	ein Freund (m), eine Freundin (f)
mate, pal	ein Kumpel
boy/girl	ein Junge/ein Mädchen
bloke, guy	ein Kerl, ein Typ
someone	jemand
has...	hat...
long hair	lange Haare
short	kurze
fair/dark	helle/dunkle
curly/straight	lockige/glatte
brown eyes	braune Augen
he/she is...	er/sie ist...
tall	groß
short	klein
fat	dick
thin	dünn

pretty/ugly	hübsch/häßlich
OK (looks)	okay
good-looking	gutaussehend
not good-looking	nicht gutaussehend
a bit, a little	etwas, ein wenig
very	sehr
so, really	so, wirklich
completely	völlig, total
nice, OK	nett
horrible, nasty	gemein
trendy, right on	in, immer vornedran
old-fashioned, square	altmodisch, out
someone past it, wrinkly	Gruftie*
clever	clever
thick	blöd
boring	langweilig
shy	schüchtern

Making the first move

Willst du was trinken?
Do you want a drink?

Wie ist deine Telefonnummer?
What's your telephone number?

Kennst du jemanden hier?
Do you know anyone here?

Hast du Lust zu tanzen?
Do you want to dance?

He's a good laugh.	I like him.	He's tall.
	I can't stand her.	She's quite pretty.

mad, crazy	verrückt	an idiot, a prat	ein Trottel
weird	seltsam	in a bad mood	schlechtgelaunt
lazy	faul	in a good mood	gutgelaunt
laid back	entspannt, locker	upset	betrübt, aufgebracht
up-tight	verklemmt	hassled, annoyed	sauer
mixed up, untogether	durcheinander, angeschlagen	depressed	down*, deprimiert
		happy	glücklich
selfish	egoistisch	Have you heard...?	Hast du gehört...?
jealous	neidisch	Petra is going out with Klaus.	Petra geht mit Klaus.
rude	unhöflich		
macho	macho	Stefan got off with Christa.	Stefan hat Christa aufgerissen*.
a bit smooth	etwas schleimig		
stuck up	eingebildet	He/she kissed me.	Er/Sie hat mich geküßt.
sloaney	schickimicky	They split up.	Sie haben sich getrennt.
yuppie	ein Yuppie		
cool	cool*, stark*	We had a row.	Wir haben uns gestritten.
a creep	ein fieser Typ		

Können wir uns mal treffen?
Can I see you again?

Kann ich auch kommen?
Can I come too?

Tut mir leid, ich kann nicht.
Sorry I can't.

Möchtest du mitkommen?
Want to come?

Vielleicht ein andermal.
Maybe some other time.

sport	Sport	twice a week	zweimal pro Woche
game, match	ein Spiel	I play...	ich spiele...
doubles	Doppel	I don't play...	ich spiele nicht...
singles	Einzel		
race	ein Rennen	tennis	Tennis
marathon	ein Marathon	squash	Squash
championships	die Meisterschaften	badminton	Federball
Olympics	die Olympischen Spiele	handball	Handball
World cup	die Fußballwelt-meisterschaft	football	Fußball
		American football	ameri-kanisches Football
club	ein Klub, ein Verein	basketball	Basketball
team	die Mannschaft	volleyball	Volleyball
referee	der Schiedsrichter	table tennis	Tischtennis
supporter	ein Fan	cricket	Kricket
training, practice	das Training	baseball	Baseball
a goal	ein Tor	I do...	ich mache...
to lose	verlieren	judo	Judo
a draw	unentschieden	karate	Karate
sports centre	ein Sportzentrum	aerobics	Aerobic
stadium	das Stadion	I go (to)...	ich gehe (zum)...[1]
court	ein Platz		
indoor	Hallen-...	I don't go (to)...	ich gehe nicht (zum)...[1]
indoor pool	ein Hallenbad		
outdoor	im Freien		
ball	ein Ball	keep-fit	Fitneß-training
net	ein Netz		
trainers	Sportschuhe	jogging	joggen
tennis shoes	Tennisschuhe	weight-training	Gewicht-training
tracksuit	ein Trainings-anzug	bowling	Bowling
once a week	einmal pro Woche	running	laufen
		I dance	ich tanze

How do you play this?	Wie spielt man das?
What are the rules?	Wie sind die Regeln?
Throw it to me.	Wirf ihn mir zu.
Catch!	Fang!
In!/Out!	In!/Aus!
You're cheating!	Du mogelst!
What team do you support?	Für welche Mannschaft bist du?
Is there a match we could go to?	Gibt es ein Spiel, zu dem wir gehen können?
Who won?	Wer hat gewonnen?

Fact file

Football is probably the most popular game in Germany. It has the biggest TV audiences, particularly for *Bundesliga* (top league) games. Tennis, cycling and windsurfing are increasingly popular. Many people play games such as volleyball and handball. Winter sports are an important pastime. Many people in the south go to the German Alps at weekends for downhill skiing. Cross-country skiing and ice-hockey are also popular.

[1]Use *zum* in front of the nouns, i.e. *Ich gehe zum Fitneßtraining/Gewichttraining/Bowling.*

Ich gehe gern
Drachenfliegen.
I love hang gliding.

Ich finde Tauchen
nicht so toll.
I'm not keen on
scuba diving.

Ich fahre lieber
Wasserski.
I prefer waterskiing.

Ich hab's nie
versucht.
I've never tried.

Ich kann nicht
schwimmen.
I can't swim.

Ist die Strömung
stark?
Are the currents
strong?

Ist das nicht
gefährlich?
It's not dangerous,
is it?

I (don't) like...	Ich gehe (nicht) gern... [1]
swimming	schwimmen
(scuba) diving	tauchen
sailing	segeln
surfing	surfen
water skiing	Wasserski laufen
canoeing	Kanufahren
rowing	rudern
I prefer...	Ich ziehe ... vor
I love...	Ich gehe besonders gern...
I (don't) like	Ich liege (nicht) gern
sunbathing.	in der Sonne.
boat	ein Boot
surfboard	ein Surfbrett
windsurfer	ein Windsurfer
boom	der Gabelbaum
mast	der Mast
sail	das Segel
sea	das Meer
beach	der Strand
pool	ein Schwimmbad
in the sun	in der Sonne
in the shade	im Schatten
goggles	eine Taucherbrille
mask	eine Tauchermaske
snorkel	ein Schnorchel
flippers	Schwimmflossen
wetsuit	ein Taucheranzug
life jacket	eine Schwimmweste
fishing	fischen
rod	eine Angel

[1]*Ich gehe gern* literally means "I go happily" or "I like going". Use it with all the sports in this word list except *Langlauf*. To say "I like cross-country skiing", say *Ich mache gern Langlauf*.

cycling	radfahren
racing bike	ein Rennrad
mountain bike	ein Mountain Bike
touring bike	ein Tourenrad
BMX	ein BMX-Rad
horse riding	reiten
horse	ein Pferd
walking, hiking	wandern
skateboarding	Skateboard fahren
skateboard	ein Skateboard
roller skating	Rollschuhlaufen
ice skating	Schlittschuhlaufen
ice hockey	Eishockey
ice rink	eine Schlittschuhbahn
skates	Schlittschuhe
skiing	Skilaufen
cross-country skiing	Langlauf[1]
ski run	die Skipiste
ski pass	eine Liftkarte
ski lift	ein Skilift
chair lift	ein Sessellift
drag lift	ein Schlepplift
skis	Skier[2]
boots	Stiefel
bindings	die Bindung
ski goggles	eine Skibrille
snow	der Schnee

[2]The Austrian word for skis is Schi.

41

I'm a student.	Ich bin Student.	French	Französisch
I'm still at school.	Ich gehe noch zur Schule.	Spanish	Spanisch
		Italian	Italienisch
I want to do...	Ich möchte gern ... studieren.	Russian	Russisch
		Latin	Latein
I do...	Ich studiere...	literature	Literatur
computing	Informatik	philosophy	Philosophie
information technology	Datenverarbeitung	sociology	Soziologie
		religious studies	Theologie
maths	Mathematik	art	Kunst
physics	Physik	drama	Theaterwissenschaften
chemistry	Chemie	crafts	Kunstgewerbe
biology	Biologie	technical drawing	Technisches Zeichnen
natural sciences	Naturwissenschaft	home economics	Hauswirtschaft(slehre)
geography	Geographie	PE	Sport
history	Geschichte		
economics	Volkswirtschaftslehre (VWL)	school	eine Schule
business studies	Betriebswirtschaftslehre (BWL)	boarding school	ein Internat
politics	Politik	public school	eine Privatschule
languages	Sprachen	(school) term	ein Halbjahr
German	Deutsch	(university) term	ein Semester
English	Englisch		

Fact file: the German system

Types of schools and colleges:[1]
—For 10 to 15 year olds, *Realschule* or *Hauptschule* (comprehensive type schools) or *Gymnasium* (grammar school) or *Gesamtschule* (combines all three).
—16 to 19 year olds doing the *Abitur* (university entrance exam) stay on in a *Gymnasium* or *Gesamtschule* for the three *Oberstufe* years (similar to sixth form).
—*Berufsschule* (for 16 to 18 year olds doing apprenticeships or job training with day release courses, or for people with the *Abitur* who are on training schemes).

—*TH* or *Technische Hochschule* (polytechnic).
—*Universität, Uni* * (university).
The school year is split into two *Halbjahre* (half years) and begins at different times in the different *Bundesländer* (states). The day begins at 7.30 or 8 and often ends at lunchtime. Schools are mixed and there is no uniform. School starts with *Erste Klasse* (first class) at age six and carries on up to *Dreizehnte* (thirteenth class). *Wehrdienst* (national service) is compulsory for men at 18 but it can be deferred while studying. *Zivildienst* (community service) can be served instead.

during term time	*während des Semesters*	teacher	*der Lehrer (m), die Lehrerin (f)*
holidays	*die Ferien*	lecturer	*der Dozent (m), die Dozentin (f)*
uniform	*eine Uniform*		
club	*ein Klub*	(language) assistant	*der Assistent (m), die Assistentin (f)*
competition	*ein Wettbewerb*		
lesson	*eine Stunde*	good	*gut*
lecture	*eine Vorlesung*	bad	*schlecht*
tuition	*Nachhilfeunterricht*	easy going	*lasch*
conversation class	*ein Kolloquium*	strict	*streng*
homework	*Hausaufgaben*	discipline	*die Disziplin*
essay	*ein Aufsatz*	to repeat (a year)	*sitzenbleiben*
translation	*eine Übersetzung*	to be expelled	*von der Schule verwiesen werden*
project	*ein Referat*		
an option	*ein Wahlfach*	to skip a lesson	*eine Stunde schwänzen*
revision	*eine Wiederholung*		
test (at school)	*eine Klassenarbeit*	to skive, to bunk off	*sich drücken*
test (college, Uni)	*eine Klausur*		
oral	*mündlich*	a grant	*ein Stipendium*
written	*schriftlich*	a loan	*ein Darlehen*
presentation	*ein Referat*	sponsorship	*Sponsorenschaft*
mark, grade	*die Note*	free	*gratis, kostenlos*

[1]The equivalents in brackets are only approximate.

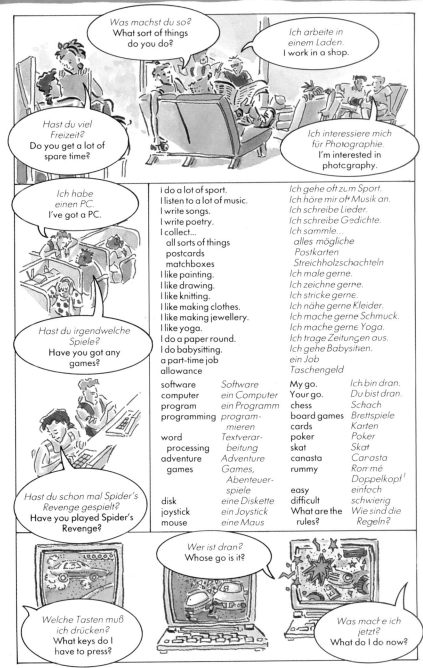

Was machst du so?
What sort of things do you do?

Ich arbeite in einem Laden.
I work in a shop.

Hast du viel Freizeit?
Do you get a lot of spare time?

Ich interessiere mich für Photographie.
I'm interested in photography.

Ich habe einen PC.
I've got a PC.

Hast du irgendwelche Spiele?
Have you got any games?

Hast du schon mal Spider's Revenge gespielt?
Have you played Spider's Revenge?

Wer ist dran?
Whose go is it?

Welche Tasten muß ich drücken?
What keys do I have to press?

Was mache ich jetzt?
What do I do now?

I do a lot of sport.	Ich gehe oft zum Sport.
I listen to a lot of music.	Ich höre mir oft Musik an.
I write songs.	Ich schreibe Lieder.
I write poetry.	Ich schreibe Gedichte.
I collect...	Ich sammle...
all sorts of things	alles mögliche
postcards	Postkarten
matchboxes	Streichholzschachteln
I like painting.	Ich male gerne.
I like drawing.	Ich zeichne gerne.
I like knitting.	Ich stricke gerne.
I like making clothes.	Ich nähe gerne Kleider.
I like making jewellery.	Ich mache gerne Schmuck.
I like yoga.	Ich mache gerne Yoga.
I do a paper round.	Ich trage Zeitungen aus.
I do babysitting.	Ich gehe Babysitten.
a part-time job	ein Job
allowance	Taschengeld

English	German	English	German
software	Software	My go.	Ich bin dran.
computer	ein Computer	Your go.	Du bist dran.
program	ein Programm	chess	Schach
programming	programmieren	board games	Brettspiele
word processing	Textverarbeitung	cards	Karten
adventure games	Adventure Games, Abenteuerspiele	poker	Poker
		skat	Skat
		canasta	Canasta
		rummy	Rommé Doppelkopf[1]
disk	eine Diskette	easy	einfach
joystick	ein Joystick	difficult	schwierig
mouse	eine Maus	What are the rules?	Wie sind die Regeln?

[1]Popular card game in Germany. [2]Countries are listed on page 55. [3]Die Grünen (the Greens) is the German Green Party but also used to mean die grüne Bewegung (the green movement).

Plans

What do you want to do later?	Was möchtest du später mal machen?
When I finish...	Wenn ich fertig bin,...
One day...	Irgendwann mal...
I want...	Ich will ...
to travel	reisen
to go to...[2]	nach . . . (gehen)
to live/work abroad	im Ausland leben/arbeiten
to have a career as...	eine Laufbahn als ... einschlagen
to get a good job	eine gute Stelle finden
to get my qualifications	meine Ausbildung abschließen
to carry on studying	weiterstudieren
I want to be a...	Ich möchte ... werden
I don't want to be a...	Ich möchte kein . . . werden

> Ich will eine Weltreise machen.
> I want to go round the world.

> Ich auch.
> So do I.

Issues

What do you think about...?	Was hältst du von . . . ?
I don't know much about...	Ich verstehe nicht viel von...
Can you explain...?	Kannst du ... erklären?
I think...	Ich glaube...
I believe in...	Ich glaube an...
I'm for...	Ich bin für...
I support...	Ich unterstütze...
I belong to...	Ich gehöre zu...
I don't believe in...	Ich glaube nicht an...
I'm against...	Ich bin gegen...
I feel angry about...	Ich bin wütend über...
That's true./Right!	Stimmt.
That's not true.	Stimmt nicht.
I agree.	Ich stimme zu.
the future	die Zukunft
(in) the past	(in der) Vergangenheit
nowadays	heutzutage
important	wichtig
religion	die Religion
god	Gott
human rights	die Menschenrechte
gay	schwul*
feminist	die Feministin
abortion	Abtreibung
drugs	Drogen
drug addict	der/die Drogenabhängige
Aids	Aids
rich, well-off	reich
poor	arm
unemployment	die Arbeitslosigkeit
Third World	die Dritte Welt
peace	der Frieden
nuclear disarmament	der Abbau von Atomwaffen
unification	die Wiedervereinigung

war	Krieg
terrorism	Terrorismus
environment	die Umwelt
conservation	die Erhaltung
ecology	die Ökologie
ozone layer	die Ozonschicht
animals	Tiere
plants	Pflanzen
trees	Bäume
deforestation	das Abholzen
acid rain	der saure Regen
pollution	die Verschmutzung
nuclear power	die Atomkraft, die Kernenergie
recycling	das Recycling
politics	die Politik
government	die Regierung
democratic	demokratisch
elections	die Wahlen
party	eine Partei
fascist	faschistisch
communist	kommunistisch
socialist	sozialistisch
green	grün[3]
conservative	konservativ
left wing	links
right wing	rechts
the left	die Linken
the right	die Rechten
radical	radikal
politically active	politisch engagiert
charity	eine Wohltätigkeitsorganisation
fund raising event	eine Wohltätigkeitsveranstaltung
demonstration, march	eine Demonstration, eine Demo

Illness, problems[1] and emergencies

doctor	ein Arzt
woman doctor	eine Ärztin
dentist	ein Zahnarzt
optician	ein Optiker
chemist[2]	eine Apotheke
pill[2]	eine Tablette, eine Pille
injection	eine Spritze
I'm allergic to...	Ich bin allergisch gegen...
antibiotics	Antibiotika
some medicines	einige Medikamente
I have...	Ich habe...
food poisoning	eine Lebens- mittelvergiftung
diarrhoea	Durchfall
cramp	einen Krampf
sunstroke	einen Hitzschlag
a headache	Kopfschmerzen
a stomach ache	Bauchschmerzen
my period	meine Tage
an infection	eine Infektion
a sore throat	Halsschmerzen
a cold	eine Erkältung
flu	eine Grippe
a toothache	Zahnschmerzen
a temperature	Fieber
a hangover	einen Kater
He/she's had too much to drink.	Er/sie hat zuviel getrunken.
I feel dizzy.	Mir ist schwindlig.
I have hayfever.	Ich leide unter Heuschnupfen.
I'm constipated.	Ich leide an Verstopfung.
I've been stung by a wasp.	Mich hat eine Wespe gestochen.
I've got mosquito bites.	Ich habe Mückenstiche.
It hurts a lot.	Es tut sehr weh.
It hurts a little.	Es tut etwas weh.
I've cut myself.	Ich habe mich geschnitten.
I think I've broken my...	Ich glaube, ich habe mir den/die/das[3]... gebrochen.
My ... hurts.	Mein/meine[4] ... tut weh.
eye	das Auge
nose	die Nase
mouth	der Mund
ear	das Ohr
chest	die Brust
arm	der Arm
hand	die Hand
wrist	das Handgelenk
finger	der Finger
leg	das Bein
knee	das Knie
ankle	der Knöchel
foot	der Fuß
bottom	das Gesäß , der Po
back	der Rücken
skin	die Haut
muscle	der Muskel

> Ich fühle mich nicht wohl.
> **I don't feel well.**

> Was fehlt dir?
> **What's wrong?**

> Ich muß mich übergeben.
> **I'm going to be sick.**

> Das tut mir sehr leid.
> **I'm really sorry about this.**

> Ich brauche einen Arzt.
> **I need to see a doctor.**

> Hat hier in der Nähe eine Apotheke auf?
> **Is there a chemist open around here?**

> Können Sie mir was gegen Heuschnupfen geben?
> **Can you give me something for hayfever?**

[1] For problems not listed here, try asking *Haben Sie ein Wörterbuch?* (Do you have a dictionary?) [2] Everyday things like plasters and aspirin are on page 24. [3] *Den* + (m) words,

Problems

Ich habe eine Kontaktlinse verloren.
I've lost my contact lens.

Jemand hat meine Sachen gestohlen.
Someone's stolen my things.

Meine Brille ist kaputt.
I've broken my glasses.

Ich habe nicht gesehen, was passiert ist.
I didn't see what happened.

my wallet	*mein Portemonnaie*	There's no water/ power.	*Es gibt kein Wasser/ keinen Strom.*
my handbag	*meine Handtasche*		
my things	*meine Sachen*		
my papers	*meine Papiere*	I'm lost.	*Ich habe mich verlaufen.*
my passport	*mein Paß*		
my key	*mein Schlüssel*	I'm in trouble.	*Ich habe ein Problem.*
all my money	*mein ganzes Geld*	I'm scared.	*Ich habe Angst.*
lost property	*das Fundbüro*	I need to talk to someone.	*Ich muß mit jemandem sprechen.*
Can you keep an eye on my things?	*Kannst du auf meine Sachen aufpassen?*	I don't know what to do...	*Ich weiß nicht, was ich machen soll...*
Has anyone seen...?	*Hat jemand...gesehen?*	I don't want to cause trouble, but...	*Ich möchte keine Umstände machen, aber...*
Please don't smoke.	*Bitte, rauchen Sie nicht.*		
Where's the socket?	*Wo ist eine Steckdose?*	A man's following me.	*Ein Mann verfolgt mich.*
It doesn't work.	*Es funktioniert nicht.*		

Fact file

In Germany everyone has to carry their identity card, so keep your passport with you. Don't be surprised if you are asked to show your *Papiere* (documents, ID).

For minor health problems or first aid treatment, the best place to go is an *Apotheke* (chemist). For something more serious you should go to a doctor or the casualty department of the local hospital. In each case you will probably have to pay. You should be able to claim back your expenses on insurance[5], but make sure you hang on to all the paperwork.

Watch out for these signs: *Notausgang* (emergency exit); *Vorsicht* (beware); *Bissiger Hund* (ferocious dog); *Betreten verboten* (keep out, no entry); *Privat* (private property); *Gefahr* (danger).

Emergencies

Emergency phone numbers: police and ambulance, 110; fire brigade, 112 (from 1992, call 112 for all three services). For very serious problems, contact the closest *Britische Konsulat* (British Consulate). Find the number in the directory.

There's been an accident.	*Es ist ein Unfall passiert.*
Help!	*Hilfe!*
Fire!	*Feuer!*
Please call...	*Bitte rufen Sie ...*
an ambulance	*einen Krankenwagen*
the police	*die Polizei*
the fire brigade	*die Feuerwehr*
a lifeguard	*einen Rettungsschwimmer*
hospital	*ein Krankenhaus*
casualty department	*die Unfallstation*
police station	*die Polizeiwache*

die + (f) and *das* + (n). See page 51. [4]*Mein* + (m) or (n) words and *meine* + (f). [5]British passport holders can use an E111 form – available from the DSS.

The German that people use every day, especially amongst friends, is different in lots of ways from correct textbook German. As in English, people use slang and have alternative ways of saying things. They also leave out bits of words (e.g. in English "I do not know" can end up sounding like "I dunno"). This book has included informal German and slang words where appropriate, but these two pages list a few of the most common words and phrases.

When using colloquial language it is easy to sound off-hand or even rude without meaning to. This is especially true for slang words, so here as in the rest of the book a single asterisk after a word shows it is mild slang, but two asterisks show it can be quite rude and it is safest not to experiment with it.

Contractions and alternative pronunciations

it	's* (es)
they, you	se* (sie)
some, a little	was* (etwas)
just	grad* (gerade)
is	is* (ist)
to have	ham* (haben)
not	nich* (nicht)
no	nee* (nein)
nothing	nix* (nichts)

Abbreviations

demonstration	eine Demo (Demonstration)
chauvinist	ein Chauvi* (Chauvinist)
frustration	der Frust* (Frustration)
teenager	ein Teenie* (Teenager)
information	die Info* (Information)
flatsharing	die WG* (Wohngemeinschaft)

American and English imports

clean; cool; down; easy; gestylt (designed); stylen (to design); Styling (design); happy; high; super; in sein (to be in); out sein (to be out); Action; Boys (blokes); Girls (girls, birds); Button (badge); Connections; Feeling; Freak (fan, freak); Fun; Horror; Kick; Look; Message; Outfit; Power; Shop; Scene or Szene; Show; Sound; Terror (riot, fun); Touch; Trouble; Workshop (class, seminar)...

Fillers

of course	logo*
(used to emphasize what follows, similar to American "man")	Mensch*
(filler word)[1]	mal
somehow	irgendwie
so, well	also
(filler: isn't it)	oder so
so, well	na ja

Slang

very, completely	absolut, irre, wahnsinnig, tierisch, total, echt, unheimlich
great, brilliant, classic	toll, spitzenmäßig, geil, stark, affengeil, klasse, heiß, voll, ultra, fetzig, scharf, astrein
lousy, bad, disgusting	schrecklich, schrott, saumäßig, ätzend
boring	stinklangweilig*
whacky, offbeat	gagig*
stupid	beknackt*
freaked out	ausgeflippt*, ausgefreakt*
bushed, hassled	gestreßt*
guy, bloke	ein Typ, ein Macker*
girl	eine Tussi**, eine Braut*
boyfriend, girlfriend	der/die Alte(r)**
parent	der/die Alte(r)**
wimp	der Softie*
gang/group of friends	die Clique*
relationship	die Beziehungskiste*
money, dough	Kies*, Knete*, Kohle*, Eier*, Mammon*
clothes, dress	Klamotten*, Fummel*
shoes	Latschen*
room	Bude*
party	Fete*
pub	Pinte*, Kneipe
quarrel, aggro	Zoff*
rubbish	Mist*
car	Karren*, Kiste*
to turn on	anturnen*
to put off	abturnen*
to cut yourself off	abblocken*
to flip, go mad	ausflippen*
to mess around	rumflippen*
to talk rubbish	schwallen*, schwafeln
to get on your nerve	nerven*
to get the hang of something	etwas checken*, etwas schnallen*
to be really keen on someone/thing	auf jemanden/etwas stehen*
to fancy someone/ something	auf jemanden/etwas abfahren*
to chat someone up	jemanden anmachen*
to sleep	ratzen*, knacken*, poofen*
to tell off	anmotzen*, anmachen*
to rip someone off	jemanden linken
It's all the same to me.	Das ist alles eine Soße.
I've got it.	Hab' ich gecheckt.* Logo.* Gebongt.*
I haven't got a clue.	Ich hab' keinen Plan.* Ich hab' keinen Dunst.*
Stay cool.	Keine Panik.*
Buzz off.	Mach die Fliege.* Putz die Platte.*

[1]This word is used a lot but does not really mean anything.

German pronunciation

To pronounce German well you need the help of a German speaker or language tapes, but these general points will help. Bear in mind that there are exceptions and strong regional variations.

Vowel sounds

a is sometimes long like "a" in arm. Sometimes it is short and sounds like the "a" in "cat" with a hint of the "u" in "cut".
ä sounds like "a" in "care".
au sounds like "ow" in "cow".
äu and *eu* sound like "oy" in "toy".
e sounds like "e" in "get" and is pronounced even when it is at the end of a word.
ei sounds like "i" in "mine".
i is sometimes short and said like "i" in "fish". When it is long it is the same as *ie* and *ih* and sounds like "ee" in "see".
ö sounds like "u" in "surf".
u sounds like "oe" in "shoe".
ü is a sharp "u" sound. Round your lips to say "oo", try to say "ee" and you will be close.
y sounds the same as *ü*.

Consonants

b at the end of a word sounds nearly like "p".
ch sounds like "ch" in the Scottish word "loch".
d sounds like an English "d" except on the ends of words when it is said like a "t".
g sounds like "g" in "good". If *ig* is at the end of a word, *g* then sounds like *ch* above.
h after a vowel is silent but makes the vowel long.
j sounds like "y" in "young".
qu sounds like "k" + "v".
r is more rolled than an English "r". On the end of a word it sounds like a short "a" sound.
s sounds like "z" in "zoo" when it comes before a vowel. Before consonants or at the end of a word, it sounds like "s" in "sort". When it is at the beginning of a word before "p" or "t", it sounds like "sh" in "short", e.g. *Stadt* (town).
sch sounds like "sh" in "short".
ß is a German letter. It sounds like "s" in "sort".
v usually sounds like "f" in "fine".
w sounds like "v" in "very".
z sounds like "ts" in "hits".

The alphabet in German

Applying the points made above, this is how you say the alphabet: Ah, Beh, C = tseh, Deh, Eh, eff, Geh, Ha, Ih, Jott, Kah, elL, emM, enN, Oh, Peh, Q = kuh, erR, esS, Teh, Uh, V = fau, Weh, X = iks, Y = üpsilon, Z = tset.

How German works

Nouns

All German nouns are written with a capital first letter. They are either masculine (m), feminine (f) or neuter (n). For a few the gender is obvious, e.g. *Mann* (man) is (m) and *Frau* (woman) is (f), but for most animals and things the gender seems random, e.g. *Zug* (train) is (m), *Fähre* (ferry) is (f), and *Auto* (car) is (n). Even with nouns for people you can't always guess the gender, e.g. *Mädchen* (girl) is (n). Some nouns have two forms, e.g. *der Lehrer/die Lehrerin* (teacher m/f).

The definite article (the word for "the") shows a noun's gender. With (m) nouns "the" is *der*, e.g. *der Zug* (the train). With (f) nouns "the" is *die*, e.g. *die Fähre* (the ferry). With (n) nouns "the" is *das*, e.g. *das Auto* (the car).

Don't worry if you muddle up *der*, *die* and *das*, you will still be understood. It is worth knowing genders of nouns since other words, particularly adjectives, change to match them, and the articles change in the different cases (see Cases). If you learn a noun, learn it with *der*, *die* or *das* (the Index lists nouns with *der*, *die* or *das)*.

Plurals

In the plural, "the" is *die*, e.g. *die Züge* (the trains). Most noun endings change in the plural and some nouns also add an umlaut (¨) over a vowel. The Index gives plural noun endings. When you learn a noun, learn its plural as well, e.g. *der Zug, die Züge.*

Cases

German nouns have four cases, or forms, depending on the job they do in a sentence. The noun ending sometimes changes and the article often changes. The four cases are: nominative – a noun is nominative when it is the subject of a sentence (the person or thing doing the action). In *Die Frau repariert das Rad* (the woman is repairing the bike), *die Frau* (the woman) is nominative; accusative – a noun is accusative when it is the direct object (the person or thing that the action directly affects). In the example above, *das Rad* (the bike) is accusative; genitive – a noun is genitive when it shows whose something is. In *Die Frau repariert das Rad des Mannes* (The woman is repairing the man's bike), *des Mannes* (the man's) is genitive;

dative – a noun is dative when it is the indirect object (the person or thing for whom something is being done). In *Die Frau gibt das Rad dem Mann* (The woman gives the bike to the man), *dem Mann* (the man) is dative.

Since *der*, *die* and *das* change with the four cases, it helps to learn them as a chart:

	(m)	(f)	(n)
singular:	the man	the woman	the child
nom	der Mann	die Frau	das Kind
acc	den Mann	die Frau	das Kind
gen	des Mannes	der Frau	des Kindes
dat	dem Mann	der Frau	dem Kind

plural:	the men	the women	the children
nom	die Männer	die Frauen	die Kinder
acc	die Männer	die Frauen	die Kinder
gen	der Männer	der Frauen	der Kinder
dat	den Männern	den Frauen	den Kindern

In everyday German the "e" in the genitive singular is dropped, e.g. *des Manns* (the man's).

Ein/eine/ein (a, an)

The indefinite article, (the word for "a") is *ein* with (m) and (n) nouns, and *eine* with (f) nouns. It also changes according to case:

	a man	a woman	a child
nom	ein Mann	eine Frau	ein Kind
acc	einen Mann	eine Frau	ein Kind
gen	eines Mannes	einer Frau	eines Kindes
dat	einem Mann	einer Frau	einem Kind

German has no plural indefinite article ("some" in English). The plural noun is used on its own, e.g. *Ich habe Äpfel* (I have apples).

Adjectives

In sentences like *Das Rad ist neu* (The bike is new), adjectives don't change. In front of a noun, e.g. *ein neues Rad* (a new bike), their ending changes to match the noun's case and gender. They change differently with "the" and "a":

Adjectives after *der/die/das* (the):

singular:	(m)	(f)	(n)
nom	der neue Film	die neue Platte	das neue Buch
acc	den neuen Film	die neue Platte	das neue Buch
gen	des neuen Films	der neuen Platte	des neuen Buchs
dat	dem neuen Film	der neuen Platte	dem neuen Buch

plural (m)/(f)/(n):

nom	die neuen Filme/Platten/Bücher
acc	die neuen Filme/Platten/Bücher
gen	der neuen Filme/Platten/Bücher
dat	den neuen Filmen/Platten/Büchern

Adjectives after *ein/eine* (a):

nom	ein neuer Film	eine neue Platte	ein neues Buch
acc	einen neuen Film	eine neue Platte	ein neues Buch
gen	eines neuen Films	einer neuen Platte	eines neuen Buchs
dat	einem neuen Film	einer neuen Platte	einem neuen Buch

In the plural they always end in "en", e.g. *neuen Filme* (new films), *neuen Platten* etc.

I, you, he, she etc.

I	ich	he	er	we	wir
you	du,	she	sie	they	sie
	Sie	it	es (also		
	or ihr		er or sie)		

There are three words for "you". *Du* is singular informal. Say *du* to a friend or someone your age or younger. *Ihr* is plural informal. Use it like *du* but when speaking to more than one person. *Sie* is polite (pol) singular and plural. Use it for strangers and older people. It is always written with a capital "S". If in doubt, use *Sie*. Saying *du* or *ihr* to people who don't expect it can be rude.

"It" is *er* when it refers to a (m) noun, *sie* when it refers to a (f) noun, and *es* when it refers to a (n) noun.

Me, you, him, it etc.

Words like "I", "you", or "it" are pronouns (words that replace nouns). In a sentence they do the same jobs as the nouns they replace, so they too have different forms in the various cases:

	I/ me[1]	you	he/ him	she/ her	it
nom	ich	du	er	sie	es
acc	mich	dich	ihn	sie	es
dat	mir	dir	ihm	ihr	ihm

	we/ us	you	you (pol)	they/ them
nom	wir	ihr	Sie	sie
acc	uns	euch	Sie	sie
dat	uns	euch	Ihnen	ihnen

My, your, his etc.

In German "my", "your" etc. change according to the noun they relate to:

with	(m)	(f)	(n) noun
my	mein	meine	mein
your	dein	deine	dein
his, its	sein	seine	sein
her, its	ihr	ihre	ihr
our	unser	unsere	unser
your	euer	eure	euer
their	ihr	ihre	ihr
your (pol)	Ihr	Ihre	Ihr

E.g. *Mein Bruder* (my brother), *meine Schwester* (my sister), etc. *Mein, dein* etc. take the same endings as *ein* in the different cases (see *Ein/eine/ein*).

[1]English pronouns also have different cases: *ich* = I, *mich* = me, *mir* = to me and so on.

Verbs

German verbs have lots of tenses (present, future etc.) but you can get by with two: the present tense for talking about the present and future, and the perfect for talking about the past.

Present tense

In German, most verbs follow one pattern. In the infinitive[1] they end in "en", e.g. *hören* (to hear). Drop "en" and use the ending you need:

I hear	ich	hör e
you hear	du/	hör st
he/she/it hears	er/ sie/es	hör t
we hear	wir	hör en
you hear	ihr	hör t
they hear	sie	hör en
you hear (pol)	Sie	hör en

Sometimes "e" precedes "t" endings, e.g. *arbeiten* (to work): *er/ihr arbeitet* (he works/you work).

Verbs like *hören* are called weak verbs. Strong verbs have a vowel change with *du* and *er*, e.g. *geben* (to give):

I give	ich	geb e
you give	du	gib st
he/she/it gives	er/ sie/es	gib t
we give	wir	geb en
you give	ihr	geb t
they give	sie	geb en
you give (pol)	Sie	geb en

Below are useful strong verbs with their *er* (he) forms in brackets. Some strong verbs only have a special past participle, a form needed for making the perfect tense (see Talking about the past), so this is given after the *er* form:

to be	*sein (ist, gewesen)*
to become	*werden (wird, geworden)*
to begin	*beginnen (beginnt, begonnen)*
to come	*kommen (kommt, gekommen)*
to do	*tun (tut, getan)*
to find	*finden (findet, gefunden)*
to go	*gehen (geht, gegangen)*
to go, to drive	*fahren (fährt, gefahren)*
to lie, to be	*liegen, (liegt, gelegen)*
to see	*sehen (sieht, gesehen)*
to stand, to be	*stehen (steht, gestanden)*
to stay	*bleiben (bleibt, geblieben)*

German doesn't distinguish between the two English present tenses (e.g. I drive, I am driving) so *ich fahre* can mean either.

Useful irregular verbs

to be[2]	*sein*	to have/ have got	*haben*
I am	*ich bin*	I have	*ich habe*
you are	*du bist*	you have	*du hast*
he/she/it is	*er/sie/es ist*	he/she/it has	*er/sie/es hat*
we are	*wir sind*	we have	*wir haben*
you are	*ihr seid*	you have	*ihr habt*
they are	*sie sind*	you have	*sie haben*
you (pol) are	*Sie sind*	you (pol) have	*Sie haben*

to have to	*müssen*	to be able to	*können*
I must	*ich muß*	I can	*ich kann*
you must	*du mußt*	you can	*du kannst*
he/she/it must	*er/sie/es muß*	he/she/it can	*er/sie/es kann*
we must	*wir müssen*	we can	*wir können*
you must	*ihr müßt*	we can	*wir können*
they must	*sie müssen*	you can	*ihr könnt*
you (pol) must	*Sie müssen*	they can	*sie können*
		you (pol) can	*Sie können*

to want to/ intend to	*wollen*
I want to	*ich will*
you want to	*du willst*
he/she/it wants to	*er/sie/es will*
we want to	*wir wollen*
you want to	*ihr wollt*
they want to	*sie wollen*
you (pol) want to	*Sie wollen*

The last three verbs are handy for making sentences like *Ich muß einen Rucksack kaufen* (I must buy a backpack), *Ich will mit dem Zug fahren* (I want to go by train). The second verb in the sentences (*kaufen* — to buy, *fahren* — to go) is in the infinitive[2] and goes at the end.

Mögen (to like) is another useful irregular verb. The present is used with a noun to say what you like, e.g. *Ich mag Horrorfilme* (I like horror films). Another form is very often used with an infinitive like the verbs above to say what you'd like to do, e.g. *Ich möchte ins Kino gehen* (I'd like to go to the cinema):

I like	*ich mag*	I'd like	*ich möchte*
you like	*du magst*	you'd like	*du möchtest*
he/she/it likes	*er/sie/es mag*	he/she/it would like	*er/sie/es möchte*
we like	*wir mögen*	we'd like	*wir möchten*
you like	*ihr mögt*	you'd like	*ihr möchtet*
they like	*sie mögen*	they'd like	*sie möchten*
you like (pol)	*Sie mögen*	you'd like (pol)	*Sie möchten*

[1]The infinitive (e.g. in English "to run", "to have") is the form in which verbs are given in the Index and in dictionaries. [2]German often uses *stehen* (to stand, to be) and *liegen* (to lie, to be) instead of *sein* for saying where things are, e.g. *Die Flasche steht auf dem Tisch* (The

Talking about the future

In everyday German the present is used, often with *später* (later), *morgen* (tomorrow) etc. to place the action in the future: *Er kauft sich morgen ein Rad* (He's going to buy himself a bike tomorrow, literally "He buys himself etc.").

Talking about the past

The easiest way to talk about the past is to use the perfect tense, e.g. *ich habe getanzt* which can mean "I danced" or "I have danced". It is made with the present of *haben* (to have) + the verb's past participle.

The past participle is made with "ge" + the verb's stem (infinitive[1] less "en" ending) + t, e.g. *hören* (to hear), *gehört* (heard); *tanzen* (to dance), *getanzt* (danced). Past participles go at the end of the sentence, e.g. *Ich habe Fußball gespielt* (I played football).

Some verbs have irregular past participles, e.g. *gehen, gegangen* (to go, went). The most useful are in the list of strong verbs (see Present tense).

Some verbs involving movement or change form the perfect with *sein* (to be), e.g. *er ist gegangen* (he has gone):[3]

to be	*sein (ist, gewesen)*
to become	*werden (wird, geworden)*
to come	*kommen (kommt, gekommen)*
to go/drive	*fahren (fährt, gefahren)*
to stay	*bleiben (bleibt, geblieben)*

Separable verbs

Many common verbs are made of two separate parts: prefix + verb, e.g. *auf + machen* (to make) = *aufmachen* (to open). In the infinitive[1], the prefix stays in place: *aufmachen* (to open). In the present tense it goes to the end of the sentence: *ich mache die Tür auf* (I open the door). In the perfect tense it goes to the start of the past participle: *ich habe die Tür aufgemacht* (I have opened the door).

Here are common prefixes with their usual meanings. Verbs that begin with one of these are separable:

ab	(off)	*nach*	(after)
an	(at, on)	*vor*	(before)
auf	(up)	*weg*	(away)
aus	(out)	*zu*	(to)
ein	(in, into)	*zurück*	(back)

Negatives

To make a sentence negative, put *nicht* (not) after the verb, e.g. *ich will nicht* (I don't want to) or with a separable verb: *ich höre nicht zu* (I'm not listening). In the perfect *nicht* precedes the past participle: *Ich habe es nicht getan* (I didn't do it).

To say "not a" you use *kein*, e.g. *Sie ist keine gute Sängerin* (She's not a good singer), *sie hat keine gute Stimme* (she hasn't got a brilliant voice, literally "She has not a brilliant voice"). *Kein* is the negative of *ein* (a) and changes like it, e.g. *kein Mann* (no man), *keine Frau* (no woman) etc. (see *Ein, eine, ein* on page 51).

Other useful negative words include *nie* (never), *niemand* (nobody) and *nichts* (nothing).

Questions

To make questions, you put the subject after the verb, e.g. *Bist du müde?* (Are you tired?) *Haben wir Zeit?* (Do we have time?)

Questions can also begin with words like:

how?	*wie?*	where?	*wo?*
how much?	*wieviel?*	which?	*welche?*
what?	*was?*	who?	*wer?*
when?	*wann?*	why?	*warum?*

Prepositions

Prepositions ("with", "on" etc.) are followed by an accusative or dative noun (or pronoun). Some always require the same case, e.g. *ohne* + accusative: *Er ist ohne mich gegangen* (He went without me); *mit* + dative: *Er ist mit mir gegangen* (He went with me). Many prepositions require either the accusative or the dative depending on whether they are indicating movement or static position. When indicating movement, they are followed by the accusative, e.g. *Er ist auf den Tisch gesprungen* (He leapt on the table). When indicating static position (no movement), they require the dative: *Er sitzt auf dem Tisch* (He's sitting on the table).

Here are some useful prepositions with the cases they require:

against	*gegen* (acc)
away from	*weg von* (dat)
behind	*hinter* (acc or dat)
beside	*neben* (acc or dat)
between	*zwischen* (acc or dat)
in	*in* (dat)
in front of	*vor* (acc or dat)
into	*in* (acc)
near	*nahe an* (dat)
on	*auf* (acc or dat)
opposite	*gegenüber* (dat)
out of	*aus* (dat)
over	*über* (acc or dat)
under	*unter* (acc or dat)
through	*durch* (acc)
with	*mit* (dat)
without	*ohne* (acc)

bottle is on the table), *Das Kino liegt an der Ecke* (The cinema is on the corner). [3]In South Germany, Austria and Switzerland, people form the perfect tense with *sein* for lots of verbs.

Numbers, colours, countries etc.

Numbers

0	*null*	15	*fünfzehn*	90	*neunzig*
1	*eins*	16	*sechzehn*	100	*(ein) hundert*
2	*zwei*	17	*siebzehn*	101	*hunderteins*
3	*drei*	18	*achtzehn*	120	*hundertzwanzig*
4	*vier*	19	*neunzehn*	121	*hunderteinundzwanzig*
5	*fünf*	20	*zwanzig*	200	*zweihundert*
6	*sechs*	21	*einundzwanzig*	300	*dreihundert*
7	*sieben*	22	*zweiundzwanzig*	1000	*(ein) tausend*
8	*acht*	30	*dreißig*	1,100	*tausendeinhundert*
9	*neun*	31	*einunddreißig*	2,000	*zweitausend*
10	*zehn*	40	*vierzig*	10,000	*zehntausend*
11	*elf*	50	*fünfzig*	100,000	*hunderttausend*
12	*zwölf*	60	*sechzig*	1,000,000	*eine Million*
13	*dreizehn*	70	*siebzig*		
14	*vierzehn*	80	*achtzig*		

Colours

colour	*die Farbe*
light	*hell*
dark	*dunkel*
black	*schwarz*
blue	*blau*
brown	*braun*
navy	*marineblau*
green	*grün*
grey	*grau*
orange	*orange(farben)*
pink	*rosa*
purple	*lila, violett*
red	*rot*
white	*weiß*
yellow	*gelb*

Seasons and weather

season	*die Jahreszeit*	autumn	*der Herbst*
spring	*der Frühling*	winter	*der Winter*
summer	*der Sommer*		

What's the weather like?	*Wie ist das Wetter?*
weather forecast	*die Wettervorhersage*
It's fine.	*Es ist schön.*
It's sunny.	*Es ist sonnig.*
It's hot.	*Es ist heiß.*
It's horrible.	*Es ist scheußlich.*
It's cold.	*Es ist kalt.*
It's windy.	*Es ist windig.*
It's raining.	*Es regnet.*
It's snowing.	*Es schneit.*
It's foggy.	*Es ist neblig.*
It's icy.	*Es hat Glatteis.*

sky	*der Himmel*
sun	*die Sonne*
clouds	*die Wolken*
rain	*der Regen*
umbrella	*der (Regen)schirm*
waterproof	*die Regenhaut*

Time

hour	*die Stunde*	evening	*der Abend*
minute	*die Minute*	midday	*Mittag*
morning	*der Morgen*	midnight	*Mitternacht*
afternoon	*der Nachmittag*		

What time is it?	*Wie spät ist es?/ Wieviel Uhr ist es?*
It's 1 o'clock.	*Es ist ein Uhr.*
2 o'clock	*zwei Uhr*
a quarter past two	*viertel nach zwei*
half past two	*halb drei*
a quarter to two	*viertel vor zwei*
five past three	*fünf nach drei*
ten to four	*zehn vor vier*
What time...?	*Wann...?/Um wieviel Uhr...?*
in ten minutes	*in zehn Minuten*

half an hour ago	*vor einer halben Stunde*
at 09 00	*um neun Uhr*
at 13.17	*um dreizehn Uhr siebzehn*
at 8 a.m.	*um acht Uhr morgens*
at 3 p.m.	*um drei Uhr nachmittags*
at 8 p.m.	*um acht Uhr abends*

Days and dates

Monday	*Montag*	March	*März*
Tuesday	*Dienstag*	April	*April*
Wednesday	*Mittwoch*	May	*Mai*
Thursday	*Donnerstag*	June	*Juni*
		July	*Juli*
Friday	*Freitag*	August	*August*
Saturday	*Samstag*	September	*September*
Sunday	*Sonntag*	October	*Oktober*
		November	*November*
January	*Januar*	December	*Dezember*
February	*Februar*		

What's the date?	*Welches Datum haben wir?*
on Monday	*am Montag*
every Monday	*montags*
in August	*im August*
1st April	*der erste April*
23rd November	*der dreiundzwanzigste November*
9th September	*der neunte September*

1990	*neunzehnhundertneunzig*
1991	*neunzehnhunderteinundneunzig*
1999	*neunzehnhundertneunundneunzig*

day	*der Tag*	today	*heute*
week	*die Woche*	tomorrow	*morgen*
month	*der Monat*	the next day	*am nächsten Tag*
year	*das Jahr*		
diary	*ein Taschenkalender*	last week	*letzte Woche*
		this week	*diese Woche*
calendar	*ein Kalender*	next week	*nächste Woche*
yesterday	*gestern*		

Countries, continents, nationalities

world	die Welt	East Germany,	Ostdeutsch-	Switzerland	(die) Schweiz
continent	der Kontinent	German	land, die	Turkey	(die) Türkei
country	das Land	Democratic	Deutsche	United States	(die) Vereinig-
border	die Grenze	Republic	Demo-		ten Staaten
north	Norden		kratische	USSR	(die) UDSSR
south	Süden		Republik	Wales	Wales
east	Osten	Great Britain	Großbritannien	Yugoslavia	Jugoslawien
west	Westen	Greece	Griechenland		
		Grenada	Grenada		
Africa	Afrika	Holland	Holland		
Asia	Asien	Hungary	Ungarn		
Australia	Australien	India	Indien		
Austria	Österreich	Ireland	Irland		
Belgium	Belgien	Israel	Israel		
Canada	Kanada	Italy	Italien		
Caribbean	(die) Karibik	Jamaica	Jamaika		
Central	Mittelamerika	Japan	Japan		
America		Kenya	Kenya		
China	China	Middle East	der Nahe Osten		
Czecho-	(die) Tschecho-	Netherlands	(die) Nieder-		
slovakia	slowakei		lande		
England	England	New Zealand	Neuseeland		
Europe	Europa	Poland	Polen		
France	Frankreich	Portugal	Portugal		
Germany	Deutschland	Russia	Rußland		
West Germany,	Westdeutsch-	Scandinavia	Skandinavien		
Federal	land, die	Scotland	Schottland		
Republic of	Bundes-	South America	Südamerika		
Germany	republik	Spain	Spanien		

The easiest way to say where you come from is to say *Ich bin aus* (I am from) or *Ich komme aus (I come from)* + name of country, e.g. *Ich bin aus Schottland* (I am from Scotland).

Faiths and beliefs

agnostic	Agnostiker
atheist	Atheist
Buddhist	Buddhist
Catholic	katholisch
Christian	Christ
Hindu	Hindu
Jewish	Jude
Muslim	Moslem, Mohamedaner
Protestant	evangelisch
Sikh	Sikh

Fact file

This Fact file supplies information on Austria and Switzerland. It focuses on the essential, practical facts that differ from information given for Germany.

Austria

Travel – Trains are run by the *ÖBB* (Austrian Federal Railways). Buses are run by the post office. Cheap deals include the *Rabbit Card* for anyone under 26, valid on railways, buses and steamer services. For local transport in cities, buy blocks of tickets from a *Tabak Trafik* (tobacconists) which work out cheaper than single tickets. Bikes can be hired from railway stations in tourist areas from April to November. Mopeds can be ridden from age 16. There are tolls on some motorways, mountain roads and tunnels.

Banks, post offices, phones – The currency is the Austrian *Schilling* (ÖS). 1 ÖS = 100 *Groschen*. Banking hours vary but are usually 8-12.30 and 1.30-3 on weekdays. In cities banks may stay open late on Thursday; some may open on Saturday. Phones take coins or cards.

Shopping – Shops open 8-6 on weekdays and 8-12 on Saturday. Many close for lunch 12-2.

Emergencies – Phone numbers: police, 133; fire, 122; ambulance, 144.

Switzerland

Languages – The three official languages are French, German and Italian.

Travel – Cheap rail deals include *Swiss Pass, Swiss Card* and *Swiss Flexi Pass*. These also entitle you to reductions on most bus and lake steamer services. The *PTT* (post office) runs bus services to remote areas; multiple-journey tickets work out cheaper. Some cities have a system of cheap day tickets for local transport. You can hire bikes from train stations but you must book the day before. You have to be 18 to ride a moped. To use motorways you need a *Vignette* (tax sticker) which you can buy at the border.

Banks, post offices, phones – The currency is the Swiss *Franc* (SF). 1 SF = 100 *Rappen*[1]. Banking hours vary. In cities banks open 8.30-4.30 on weekdays, elsewhere they close for lunch from 12-2. Chain stores, e.g. *Migros* and *Co-op*, often change money. Phone boxes mainly take coins.

Shopping – Opening times vary a lot. Shops tend to open earlier than in Germany, but some are closed on Monday mornings.

Emergencies – There is no national health service so make sure you are insured. Phone numbers: police, 117; fire, 118; ambulance, 144.

[1]The French word *Centimes* is sometimes used instead of *Rappen*.

Index

This Index lists the most essential words. If you can't find the word you want, look up a relevant entry, e.g. to find "onion", look under "vegetables". Nouns have their plurals in brackets: (¨) means the plural has an umlaut, (-) means it doesn't change (see page 50). Verbs are in the infinitive (see page 52).

to bunk off, 43	sich drücken
bus, 6, 7	der Bus(se)
bus station, 7	der Busbahnhof(¨e)
bus stop, 7	die Bushaltestelle(n)
to be busy, 30	keine Zeit haben
butter, 20	die Butter
to buy, 6	kaufen
bye, 3	tschüs
cable TV, 33	das Kabelfernsehen
café, 16-17	das Café(s)
cake, 16	der Kuchen(-)
(telephone) call, 13	das Gespräch(e)
to call, 13, 15	anrufen
to call back, 15	zurückrufen
calm, 8	ruhig
to camp, 10	zelten
camping, 10-11	das Camping
campsites, 10	der Campingplatz(¨e)
to cancel, 8	stornieren
can opener, 11	der Dosenöffner(-)
car, 9	das Auto(s)
parts of, 9	
caravan, 11	der Wohnwagen(-)
career, 45	die Laufbahn(en)
car park, 5	der Parkplatz(¨e)
carrier bag, 25	die Tragetasche(n)
to carry	tragen
cashier's desk, 15	die Kasse(n)
cassette, 28	die Kassette(n)
castle, 30	das Schloß(¨sser)
casualty department, 47	die Unfallstation(en)
to catch, 39	fangen
cathedral, 30	der Dom(e)
chair, 16	der Stuhl(¨e)
to change, 6, 8	ändern
changing room, 27	die Umkleidekabine(n)
channel (TV), 33	das Programm(e)
charter flight, 8	der Charterflug(¨e)
charts (music), 29	die Hitparade(n), Charts (pl)
cheap, 11	billig
to cheat, 39	mogeln
to check in, 8	einchecken
check-out, 22	die Kasse(n)
Cheers!, 15	Prost!
cheese, 16, 18	der Käse(-)
chemist, 22, 46	die Apotheke(n), die Drogerie(n)
chicken, 21	das Hähnchen(-)
chips, 18	die Fritten (f pl), Pommes frites
chocolate, 25	die Schokolade(n)
church, 5, 30	die Kirche(n)
cigarette	die Zigarette(n)
cinema, 5, 30, 33	das Kino(s)
clean, 11	sauber
clever, 36	clever*
closed, 22	geschlossen
clothes, 26-27	die Kleider
club, 30	die Disco(s)

club (sports), 39	der Klub(s), der Verein(e)
coach (bus), 7	der Bus(se)
(telephone) code, 14	die Vorwahl
coffee, 16	der Kaffee
coke, 16	das Cola
cold, 11, 13	kalt
a cold, 46	die Erkältung(en)
to collect, 44	sammeln
college, 42	die Hochschule(n)
types of, 43	
colour, 24, 26, 54	die Farbe(n)
to come, 37	kommen
comic, 33	das Comic(s)
commercial, 33	kommerziell
compact disc, 28	die CD(s)
completely, 36	völlig, total
computer, 44	der Computer(-)
concert, 29	das Konzert(e)
to confirm, 8	bestätigen
to be constipated, 46	an Verstopfung leiden
contact lens, 47	die Kontaktlinse(n)
cool, 27, 37	cool, stark*
corner, 5	die Ecke(n)
to cost	kosten
Could I have..., 3	Ich hätte gern...
countries, 55	
countryside, 30	die Landschaft(en)
cramp, 46	der Krampf(¨e)
crash helmet, 9	der Sturzhelm(e)
crazy, 37	verrückt
credit card, 15	die Kreditkarte(n)
a creep, 37	ein fieser Typ
crisps	Chips (n pl)
to cross, 4	überqueren
crossroads, junction, 4	die Kreuzung(en)
curly, 36	lockig
currency, 15	die Währung(en)
currents, 40	die Strömung(en)
customs, 8	der Zoll
to cut oneself, 46	sich schneiden
cut price, 8	das Sonderangebot(e)
to dance, 30, 36	tanzen
danger, 47	die Gefahr(en)
dangerous, 40	gefährlich
dark (colouring)	dunkel
dates, 54	Daten (n pl)
day, 54	der Tag(e)
day after tomorrow, 30, 54	übermorgen
days of the week, 54	Wochentage (m pl)
dead end, 5	die Sackgasse(n)
delay, 8	die Verspätung(en)
delicious, 21	köstlich
demo, 45	die Demonstration(en), die Demo(s)
dentist, 46	der Zahnarzt(¨e)
deodorant, 12	der Deo(dorant)(s)
department store, 22	das Kaufhaus(¨er)
departure gate, 8	der Ausgang(¨e)
departures, 7	Abfahrt, Abflug

depressed, 37	down*, deprimiert	exit, 22	der Ausgang(¨e)
dessert, 18	die Nachspeise(n),	to expect, 15	erwarten
	der Nachtisch(e)	to be expelled, 43	von der Schule
diarrhoea, 46	der Durchfall		verwiesen werden
dictionary, 46	das Wörterbuch(¨er)	expensive, 11, 41	teuer
difficult, 44	schwierig	to explain, 45	erklären
dinner, 11, 21	das Abendessen(-)	extra, 13	noch ein/eine
(film) director, 33	der Regisseur(e)	eye, 36	das Auge(n)
(telephone) directory,	das Telefonbuch(¨er)		
15		fair (colouring)	hell
discipline, 43	die Disziplin	family, 35	die Familie(n)
disco, 30	die Disco(s)	fan (music), 29	der Fan(s)
divorced, 35	geschieden	fantastic, 27	super*, stark*
dizzy, 46	schwindlig	far, 5	weit
to do, 34	machen	fare, 7	der Fahrpreis(e)
to do (study), 42, 43	studieren	fashion, 27	die Mode(n)
doctor, 46	der Arzt(¨e)/die	fashionable, 27	modisch, in*
	Ärztin(nen)	fat, 36	dick
(car) documents, 9	die Wagenpapiere (pl)	father, 35	der Vater(¨)
doubles, 39	das Doppel(-)	to be fed up	genug haben
doughnut, 25	der Berliner(-)	feminist, 45	die Feministin(nen)
downstairs, 13	unten	ferry, 8	die Fähre(n)
a draw (sports), 39	unentschieden	film (camera), 24	der Film(e)
to draw, 4	aufzeichnen	film (cinema), 31,	der Film(e)
(salad) dressing, 18	die Salatsoße(n)	32-33	
dressy, 27	aufgedonnert	film buff, 33	der Kinofan(s)
to drink, 11, 16	trinken	to finish, 30, 42	aufhören, fertig sein
drinks, types of, 16-17		Fire!, 47	Feuer!
to go for a drink, 30	etwas trinken gehen	fire brigade, 47	die Feuerwehr
drinking water, 11, 47	das Trinkwasser	fireworks, 30	das Feuerwerk(e)
to drive	Auto fahren	first, 4	erste
driving licence, 9	der Führerschein(e)	fish, 18	der Fisch(e)
drugs, 45	Drogen (f pl)	to fix, 9	reparieren
to dry, 12	trocknen	flat (apartment), 35	die Wohnung(en)
dubbed, 33	synchronisiert	flea market, 22	der Flohmarkt(¨e)
dull, boring, 30	langweilig	flight, 8	der Flug(¨e)
		flight number, 8	die Flugnummer(n)
easy, 44	einfach	floor, 13	der Boden(¨)
easy going, 43	lasch	flu, 46	die Grippe(n)
to eat, 16	essen	to follow, 4, 47	folgen, verfolgen
eating, 16-17, 18-19,		food, 16, 18-19,	Essen
20-21		21, 23, 25	
egg, 21	das Ei(er)	food poisoning, 46	die Lebensmittel-
electric socket, 13	die Steckdose(n)		vergiftung(en)
emergencies, 47		foot passenger, 8	der Passagier(e)
emergency exit, 47	der Notausgang(¨e)	foreign exchange, 15	Devisen, Wechsel
end of, at the end, 5	am Ende	foreign exchange	die Wechselstube(n)
engine, 9	der Motor(en)	office, 15	
English, 3, 55	Englisch	forest	der Wald(¨er)
enough, 25	genug	fork, 21	die Gabel(n)
enquiries, 15	Auskunft, Information	fountain, 31	der Brunnen(-)
entertainment guide,	das Programm(e)	free (empty), 16	frei
30		free (without charge),	gratis, kostenlos
entrance, 22	der Eingang(¨e)	43	
environment, 45	die Umwelt	friend, 36	der Freund(e)/die
evening, 13, 30, 54	abends		Freundin(nen)
every day, 7	täglich	fruit, 18, 25	das Obst
exam, 43	das Examen(-)	fruit juice, 16	der Fruchtsaft(¨e)
except, 7	außer	fruit/veg stall, 22	der Obst- und
exchange rate, 15	der Wechselkurs(e)		Gemüsehändler(-)
exciting, 33	aufregend, spannend	full, 10	belegt
excuse me, 3, 19	entschuldigen Sie,	funny, 33	lustig
	entschuldige, hallo	the future, 45	die Zukunft
exhibition, 30	die Ausstellung(en)		

game, 38, 39, 44	das Spiel(e)
garage, 9	die Werkstatt(¨en)
garlic, 21	der Knoblauch
gay, 45	schwul
gear, 9	der Gang(¨e)
(hair) gel, 24	das Gel(s), das Haargel(s)
German, 3	Deutsch
gig, 29	der Gig(s), der Auftritt(e)
girl, 36	das Mädchen(-)
girlfriend, 35	die Freundin(nen)
glass, 16	das Glas(¨er)
glasses, 47	die Brille(n)
to go, 4	gehen
to go out with, 37	gehen mit
a goal, 39	das Tor(e)
god, 45	der Gott(¨er)
goggles, 40	die Taucherbrille(n)
good, 33, 43	gut
goodbye, 3, 13	auf Wiedersehen
good-looking, 36	gutaussehend
not good-looking, 36	nicht gutaussehend
in a good mood, 37	gutgelaunt
gossip, 36-37	der Klatsch
grant (student), 43	das Stipendium (Stipendien)
greengrocer, 22	der Obst- und Gemüsehändler(-)
greetings, 3, 12	
group (musicians), 29	die Gruppe(n), die Band(s)
guide book, 30	der Reiseführer(-)
guy, 36	der Kerl(s), der Typ(en)
hair, 36	die Haare (n pl)
hairdryer, 12	der Fön(s)
ham, 16	der Schinken(-)
hamburger, 18	der Hamburger(-)
handbag, 47	die Handtasche(n)
hand luggage, 8	das Handgepäck
hang on, 15	bleib' am Apparat
hangover, 46	der Kater(-)
happy, 37	glücklich
hassled, 37	sauer
to have, 3, 52	haben
hayfever, 46	der Heuschnupfen(-)
headache, 46	die Kopfschmerzen (m pl)
headphones, 28	die Kopfhörer (m pl)
health food shop, 22	das Reformhaus(¨er)
to hear, 29	hören
heavy, 8	schwer
hello, 3, 12	hallo, Guten Tag
Help!, 47	Hilfe!
to help, 4, 20	helfen
here, 5, 34	hier
Hi, 3	Hi, Hallo
hi-fi, 28	die Stereo-Anlage(n)
to hire, 9	vermieten
bikes and mopeds, 9	
skis, 41	
hit (music), 29	der Hit(s)

to hitch, 9	trampen
holiday, 35, 43	die Ferien
homework, 43	Hausaufgaben (f pl)
horrible, 36	gemein
hospital, 47	das Krankenhaus(¨er)
hot, 11	warm, heiß
(too) hot, spicy, 21	(zu) scharf
hot chocolate, 16	die heiße Schokolade(n)
hotel, 10	das Hotel(s)
house, 35	das Haus(¨er)
hovercraft, 8	das Hovercraft(s)
How?, 3	Wie?
How are you?, 12	Wie geht es Ihnen?
How long? (time), 34	Wie lange?
How many?, 3	Wieviele?
How much?, 3	Wieviel?
How much is it?, 3, 22	Was kostet das?
How often?, 38	Wie oft?
to be hungry, 21	Hunger haben
to hurt a little, 46	etwas weh tun
to hurt a lot, 46	sehr weh tun
husband, 35	der Mann(¨er)
(with) ice, 16	mit Eis
ice-cream, 16	das Eis
ID, 47	Papiere
idea, 30	die Idee(n)
idiot, 37	der Trottel(-)
I'd like..., 3	Ich möchte...
important, 45	wichtig
ill	krank
illness, 46-47	
I'm in trouble., 47	Ich habe ein Problem.
I'm lost., 47	Ich habe mich verlaufen.
in, 5	in
indoor, 39	Hallen-...
infection, 46	die Infektion(en)
information, 8	die Auskunft
in front of, 5	vor
injection, 46	die Spritze(n)
(musical) instrument, 29	das Instrument(e)
insurance, 9, 47	die Versicherung(en)
interesting, 30	interessant
interests, 44	
Is there...?, 3	Gibt es...?
It/this is..., 3	Das ist...
jacket, 27	die Jacke(n)
jam, 21	die Konfitüre(n)
jealous, 37	neidisch
jeans, 26	Jeans (f pl)
job, 45	die Stelle(n)
journey, 6	die Fahrt(en)
junction, crossroads, 4	die Kreuzung(en)
Keep out!, 47	Betreten verboten!
ketchup, 18	das Tomatenketchup
key, 11, 13, 47	der Schlüssel(-)
to kiss, 37	küssen
knife, 21	das Messer(-)
to know, 3, 36	wissen, kennen

laid-back, 37	entspannt, locker
lake, 30	der See(n)
language, 42	die Sprache(n)
large	groß
last, 7	letzte
later, 45	später
latest, 7	neuste
launderette, 22	der Waschsalon(s)
to lay the table, 20	den Tisch decken
lazy, 37	faul
to learn, 29	lernen
to leave (depart), 7	abfahren
to leave (a message), 15	hinterlassen (eine Nachricht)
lecture, 43	die Vorlesung(en)
lecturer, 43	der Dozent(en)/die Dozentin(nen)
left, 4	links
left luggage locker, 7	Schließfächer (n pl)
lemon, 16	die Zitrone(n)
a slice of, 16	eine Scheibe
less, 25	weniger
lesson, 43	die Stunde(n)
letter, 15	der Brief(e)
library, 33	die Bücherei(en)
lifeguard, 47	der Rettungs-schwimmer(-)
to like	gern haben
to like (doing)	gern tun
to listen, 28	hören
litre, 9	der Liter(-)
a little, 20	ein wenig, etwas
live (music), 29	live Musik
to live, 34, 35	wohnen
to live with, 35	zusammenwohnen mit
liver, 21	die Leber(n)
loads, 42	massenhaft
a loan, 43	das Darlehen(-)
long, 27, 36	lang
loo, 12	das Klo(s)
loo paper, 11	das Klopapier
look (style), 27	der Look
to look, 24	sich umsehen
to lose, 14, 39	verlieren
to be lost, 4	sich verlaufen haben
lost property, 47	das Fundbüro(s)
loud, 28	laut
loudspeaker, 7	der Lautsprecher(-)
lousy, 33	schrecklich
luggage, 8	das Gepäck
lunch, 11	das Mittagessen(-)
machine, 6	der Automat(en)
macho, 37	macho
mad, 37	verrückt
main street, 4	die Hauptstraße(n)
main course, 18	das Hauptgericht(e)
make-up, 24	das Make-up
man	der Mann(¨er)
map, 5	der Plan(¨e)
march, demo, 45	die Demonstration(en), die Demo(s)
margarine, 21	die Margarine
market, 22	der Markt(¨e)
married, 35	verheiratet
mask, 40	die Tauchermaske(n)
match (sports), 39	das Spiel(e)
matches, 11	Streichhölzer (n pl)
mate, 36	der Kumpel(-)
maybe, 3	vielleicht
mayonnaise, 18	die Mayonnaise
meal, 21	das Essen(-)
to mean, 3	bedeuten
meat, 18, 21	das Fleisch
medicine, 46	das Medikament(e)
medium, 27	medium
to meet, 8, 31	abholen, sich treffen
menu, 16, 19	die Karte(n)
message, 15	die Nachricht(en)
milk, 16	die Milch
milkshake, 16	der Milchshake(s)
mineral water, 16	das Mineralwasser(-)
fizzy	mit Kohlensäure
still	ohne Kohlensäure
Miss	Fräulein
mixed up, 37	durcheinander, angeschlagen
money, 14, 15, 47	das Geld
moped, 9	das Moped(s)
month, 54	der Monat(e)
more, 25	mehr
morning, 30, 54	morgens
mosquito bite, 46	der Mückenstich(e)
mother, 35	die Mutter(¨)
motorbike, 9	das Motorrad(¨er)
motorway, 5	die Autobahn(en)
mountain, 30	der Berg(e)
movie, 33	der Film(e)
Mr, Sir, 12	Herr
Mrs, 12	Frau
museum, 5, 30	das Museum (Museen)
music, 28-29	die Musik
music/pop video, 28	der Videoclip(s)
mustard, 18	der Senf
My name is..., 35	Ich heiße...
nasty, 36	gemein
nationalities, 55	
national service, 43	der Wehrdienst
near, nearby, 5	in der Nähe
new, 29	neu
news, 33	die Nachrichten (f pl)
newspaper, 24	die Zeitung(en)
next, 6, 7	nächste
next to, 5	neben
nice, 13	nett
nice (friendly), 36	nett
nickname, 35	der Spitzname(n)
night, 11	die Nacht(¨)
nightclub	die Bar(s)
no, 3, 53	nein
nobody, 53	niemand
no entry, 5, 47	keine Einfahrt, Betreten verboten
no parking, 5	Parken verboten
no smoking, 8	Nichtraucher
novel, 33	der Roman(e)
now, nowadays, 45	heutzutage

nuclear disarmament, 45	der Abbau von Atomwaffen
nuclear power, 45	die Atomkraft, die Kernenergie
number, 15	die Nummer(n)
number one (record), 29	die Nummer eins
numbers, 3, 54	Zahlen (f pl)
offbeat, 33	ungewöhnlich
oil, 9	das Öl
OK, 36	nett
OK (looks), 36	okay
old	alt
old-fashioned, 36	altmodisch, out*
omelette, 16	das Omelett(s)
on, 5	auf
one way, 5	die Einbahnstraße(n)
open, 22	geöffnet
opposite, 5	gegenüber
optician, 46	der Optiker(-)
or, 3	oder
to order, 18	bestellen
other	andere
some other time, 37	ein andermal
outdoor, 39	im Freien
out-of-date, 27	altmodisch
over, 5	über
over the top, 33	übertrieben
pal, 36	der Kumpel(-)
papers (personal), 47	die Papiere
parcel, 15	das Paket(e)
parents, 35	die Eltern
park, 5	der Park(s)
parking meter, 5	die Parkuhr(en)
part-time job, 44	der Job(s)
party, 30	die Fete(n)
passport, 8, 47 ·	der Paß (Pässe)
(in the) past, 45	(in der) Vergangenheit
pasta, 21	Nudeln (f pl)
path, footpath, 4	der Fahrradweg(e)
pavement, 5	der Bürgersteig(e)
to pay, 11	bezahlen
peace, 45	der Frieden
peanuts, 25	Erdnüsse (f pl)
pedestrian crossing, 4	der Fußgänger-überweg(e), der Zebrastreifen(-)
pedestrians, 5	Fußgänger (m pl)
pen, ballpoint, 24	der Stift(e)
people, 10	Personen (f pl)
pepper, 18	der Pfeffer
(my) period, 46	(meine) Tage
personal stereo, 28	der Walkman(s)
petrol, 9	das Benzin
petrol station, 9	die Tankstelle(n)
phone, 13, 14-15	das Telefon(e)
phone box, 13	die Telefonzelle(n)
phonecard, 15	die Telefonkarte(n)
phone number, 15	die (Telefon) nummer(n)
photography, 33, 44	die Aufnahmen (f pl), die Photographie
picnic, 30	das Picknick(s)
pill, 46	die Tablette(n), die Pille(n)
pizza, 18	die Pizza(s)
plant, 45	die Pflanze(n)
plate, 21	der Teller(-)
platform, 7	der Bahnsteig(e)
play (theatre), 33	das Stück(e), das Schauspiel(e)
to play, 29, 38	spielen
please, 3	bitte
pocket money, 44	das Taschengeld
poetry, 33	Gedichte
police, 47	die Polizei
police station, 47	die Polizeiwache(n)
political, 33	politisch
politics, 45	die Politik
pollution, 45	die Verschmutzung
poor, 45	arm
pork, 21	das Schweinefleisch
port, 8	der Hafen(¨)
postbox, 15	der Briefkasten(¨)
postcard, 15, 24	die Postkarte(n)
poste restante, 15	postlagernd
post office, 5	die Post, das Postamt(¨er)
power (electricity), 47	der Strom
to prefer, 40	etwas lieber tun
pregnant	schwanger
pretty, 36	hübsch
price, 18, 22	der Preis(e)
private property, 47	privat
problems, 47	
programme (TV), 33	die Sendung(en)
pub, 16	die Kneipe(n)
to have a puncture, 9	einen Platten haben
to put	stellen, legen
qualifications, 45	die Ausbildung
Quick!, 39	Schnell!
quite, 37	recht
racket, 38	der Schläger(-)
(car) radiator, 9	der Kühler(-)
radio, 28	das Radio(s)
radio-cassette player, 28	der Radiorecorder(-)
railway line, 5	die Eisenbahnlinie(n)
railways, 7	die Bahn
railway station, 7	der Bahnhof(¨e)
rain, 54	der Regen
raw, 21	roh
to read, 32	lesen
really, 36	so, wirklich
record player, 28	der Plattenspieler(-)
record, 28	die Platte(n)
record shop, 28	der Plattenladen(¨)
reduction, 7	die Ermäßigung(en)
region, 30	die Umgebung, die Gegend
(by) registered post, 15	(per) Einschreiben
registration form, 11	das Anmeldefor-mular(e)

religion, 45, 55	die Religion(en)
to repair, 23	reparieren
to reserve, 7	reservieren
restaurant, 11, 18-19	das Restaurant(s)
reverse charge call, 15	das R-Gespräch(e)
rice, 21	der Reis
rich, well-off, 45	reich
right, 4	rechts
right (correct), 45	stimmt
ringroad, 5	die Umgehungsstraße(n)
river, 5, 30	der Fluß (Flüsse)
road, 4	die Straße(n)
room, 10, 11	das Zimmer(-)
rough, 8	stürmisch
roundabout, 4	der Kreisverkehr
rucksack, backpack, 8	der Rucksack("e)
rude, 37	unhöflich
rule, 39	die Regel(n)
to run	rennen
sad, 33	traurig
safety pin, 27	die Sicherheitsnadel(n)
salad, 18	der Salat(e)
sale, 27	der Ausverkauf
salt, 18	das Salz
salty, 21	salzig
sandwich, 16	das (belegte) Brot
satellite TV, 33	das Satellitenfernsehen
satirical, 33	satirisch
sausage, 18	das Würstchen(-)
to say	sagen
to say again, repeat, 3	etwas noch einmal sagen
scary, 33	gruslig
school, 5, 33, 42	die Schule(n)
types of, 43	
scissors, 13	die Schere(n)
scruffy, 27	verlottert
sea, 40	das Meer(e)
seat, 7	der Sitzplatz("e)
second, 4	zweite
second-hand, 27	gebraucht
section, 28	die Abteilung(en)
to see, 11	sehen
selfish, 37	egoistisch
to sell	verkaufen
serious, 33	ernst
sex, 33	Sex
shade, 40	der Schatten
shampoo, 12	das Shampoo(s)
shopping centre	das Einkaufszentrum (zentren)
shop, 5, 11, 22-23, 24-25	der Laden("), das Geschäft(e)
short, 27, 36	kurz, klein
show (entertainment), 30	die Show(s)
to show, 5	zeigen
shower (bathroom), 12	die Dusche(n)
Shut up!, 48	Halt den Mund!
shy, 36	schüchtern
to be sick, 46	sich übergeben
silly, 33	blöde
to sing, 29	singen
single (record), 28	die Single(s)
single (unmarried), 35	single
singles, 39	Einzel
Sir, Mr, 12	Herr
sister, 35	die Schwester(n)
size, 26	die Größe(n)
skiing, 41	Skilaufen
to skive, 43	sich drücken
to sleep, 12	schlafen
sleeping bag, 13	der Schlafsack("e)
slice, 25	die Scheibe(n)
slower, 3	langsamer
small, 25	klein
small change, 15	das Kleingeld
smaller, 24, 27	kleiner
smart, 27	schick
to smoke, 47	rauchen
snacks, 16	Snacks, Imbiß
snow, 41	der Schnee
so, 36	so, wirklich
soap, 12	die Seife(n)
soap (opera), 33	die Serie(n), Soap
socket, 47	die Steckdose(n)
someone, 36	jemand
something, 32	was
song, 29	der Song(s)
sore throat, 46	Halsschmerzen (m pl)
sorry, 3	Entschuldigung
soup	die Suppe(n)
spaghetti, 18	Spaghetti
spare time, 44	die Freizeit
to speak, 3	sprechen
special offer, 8	das Sonderangebot(e)
(too) spicy, 21	(zu) scharf
to split, 26	aufplatzen
to split up, 37	sich trennen
spoon, 21	der Löffel(-)
sport, 38-39, 40-41	der Sport
sports centre, 39	das Sportzentrum (zentren)
square, 5	der Platz("e)
square (old-fashioned), 36	altmodisch, out*
stadium, 39	das Stadion (Stadien)
stairs, 22	die Treppe(n)
stamp, 15	die Briefmarke(n)
standby, 8	Standby
to start, 30	anfangen
starter, 18	die Vorspeise(n)
(radio) station, 28	der Sender(-)
(railway) station, 7	der Bahnhof("e)
to stay, 35	wohnen
steak, 18	das Steak(s)
medium	halbdurch
rare	blutig
well done	durchgebraten
to steal, 47	stehlen
to sting, 46	stechen
stomach ache, 46	die Bauchschmerzen (m pl)
straight (hair), 36	glatt
straight ahead, 4	geradeaus

street, 4	die Straße(n)
strict, 43	streng
strong, 40	stark
stuck up, 37	eingebildet
student, 42	der Student(en)/die Studentin(nen)
student fare, 7, 30	die Studentenermäßigung
to study, 35	studieren
style, 27	der Stil
subject, 42, 43	das Fach(¨er)
with subtitles, 33	mit Untertiteln
suburbs, 5	der Vorort(e), der Stadtrand
subway, 4	die Unterführung(en)
sugar, 16	der Zucker
suitcase, 8	der Koffer(-)
sun, 40	die Sonne(n)
sunbathing, 40	in der Sonne liegen
sunglasses, 23	die Sonnenbrille(n)
sunscreen, 24	das Sonnenschutzmittel(-)
sunstroke, 46	der Hitzschlag(¨e)
sun-tan lotion, 24	die Sonnencreme(s)
supermarket, 22	der Supermarkt(¨e)
to support, 45	unterstützen
surfboard, 40	das Surfbrett(er)
surname, 35	der Nachname(n)
sweet (taste), 21	süß
sweets, 25	die Süßigkeiten (f pl)
to swim, 11, 40	schwimmen
swimming pool, 11	das Schwimmbad(¨er), der Swimmingpool(s)
swimsuit/trunks, 27	der Badeanzug(¨e), die Badehose(n)
table, 16	der Tisch(e)
to take, 4	nehmen
take-away, 18	zum Mitnehmen
tall, 36	groß
tape, 28	die Kassette
to tape, 28	aufnehmen
tap water, 11	das Wasser
taxi, 8	das Taxi(s)
tea, 16	der Tee
with lemon	mit Zitrone
with milk	mit Milch
teacher, 43	der Lehrer(-)/die Lehrerin(nen)
team, 39	die Mannschaft(en)
telephone, 13, 14-15	das Telefon(e)
telephone box, 15	die Telefonzelle(n)
to tell, 15	sagen
telly, TV, 33	die Glotze(n)*
a temperature, 46	das Fieber
tent, 11	das Zelt(e)
term, 42	das Halbjahr(e), das Semester(-)
thank you, 3	danke
theatre, 33	das Theater(-)
there, 5	dort
there is, 3	es gibt
thick, 36	blöd
thin, 36	dünn
things, 12, 47	Sachen
to think about, 24	es sich überlegen
to think of, 32, 45	finden, halten von
third, 4	dritte
Third World, 45	die Dritte Welt
thirsty, 21	der Durst
to throw, 39	werfen
ticket, 6, 7, 8, 30	die Fahrkarte(n), die Karte(n)
ticket machine, 7	der Fahrkartenautomat(en)
ticket office, 7, 30	der Fahrkartenschalter(-), die Vorverkaufsstelle(n), die Theaterkasse(n)
tight, 27	eng
till, 15	die Kasse(n)
time, 54	die Zeit
timetable, 7	der Fahrplan(¨e)
tired, 13	müde
tissue, 24	das Papiertaschentuch(¨er)
today, 30, 54	heute
toilet, 12	die Toilette(n)
toilet paper, 11	das Klopapier
toilet, public, 4	die öffentliche(n) Toilette(n)
gents (sign)	Herren, Männer
ladies (sign)	Damen, Frauen
tomorrow, 30, 54	morgen
tonight, 30, 54	heute abend
too, 21, 37	zu
toothache, 46	Zahnschmerzen (m pl)
toothpaste, 12	die Zahnpasta(pasten)
the Top 10, 29	die Top Ten
tour (music), 29	die Tour(s, en)
tour (sightseeing), 30	die Tour(en), die Rundfahrt(en)
tourist office, 5, 10, 31	das Fremdenverkehrsbüro(s), der Verkehrsverein(e)
towel, 12	das Handtuch(¨er)
town	die Stadt(¨e)
centre, 5	die Stadtmitte, das Zentrum, die City
old town	die Altstadt(¨e)
town hall, 5	das Rathaus(¨er)
track (music), 28	das Stück(e)
traffic lights, 4	die Ampel(n)
train, 6, 7	der Zug(¨e)
trainers, 27, 39	die Turnschuhe (m pl), die Sportschuhe (m pl)
tram, 7	die Straßenbahn(en)
travel, 4-5, 6-7, 8-9	
to travel, 35	unterwegs sein
travel agent, 8	das Reisebüro(s)
traveller's cheques, 14, 15	Reiseschecks (m pl)
tree, 45	der Baume (¨e)
trendy, 27, 36	flott, in*, immer vornedran
trolley, 8	der Gepäckwagen(-)
trouble, 47	das Problem(e)
to try	versuchen

to try on, 26	anprobieren
to turn, 4	abbiegen
to turn down (the volume), 28	leiser drehen
TV, 33	das Fernsehen
tyre, 9	der Reifen(-)
ugly, 36	häßlich
under, 5	unter
underground station, 7	die U-Bahn-Station(en)
underground train, 7	die U-Bahn(en)
to understand, 3	verstehen
underwear, 27	die Unterwäsche
unemployment, 45	die Arbeitslosigkeit
unfit, 38	nicht fit
uniform, 43	die Uniform(en)
university, 43	die Universität(en)
untogether, 37	durcheinander, angeschlagen
upset, 37	betrübt, aufgebracht
upstairs, 13	oben
up-tight, 37	verklemmt
USA, 15, 55	Amerika
to use, 13	benutzen
veal, 21	das Kalbfleisch
vegetables, 18, 21	das Gemüse
vegetarian, 21	der Vegetarier(-)/die Vegetarierin(nen)
very, 36	sehr
video, 29, 32	das Video(s)
village	das Dorf(¨er)
violence, 33	die Gewalt
visa, 8	das Visum (Visen)
to wake somebody up, 12	jemanden wecken
to walk	(zu Fuß) gehen, laufen
Walkman, 28	der Walkman(s)
wallet, 47	das Portemonnaie(s)
to want, 3, 31	möchten, wollen
war, 45	der Krieg(e)
to wash, 12	waschen
washing powder, 12	das Waschpulver(-)
to do the washing up, 20	abwaschen
wasp, 46	die Wespe(n)
water, 11, 47	das Wasser
weather, 54	das Wetter
week, 30, 54	die Woche(n)
weird, 37	seltsam
well known, 33	bekannt
well-off, 45	reich
What?	Was?
What is it/this?, 3	Was ist das?
What's on?, 31	Was wird gespielt?
What time...?, 6, 54	Wann...?
What time is it?, 54	Wie spät ist es?

when, 3	wann
where, 3, 34	wo, woher
why, 3	warum
wife, 35	die Frau(en)
to win, 39	gewinnen
windsurfer, 40	der Windsurfer(-)
wine, 16	der Wein(e)
red	der Rotwein(e)
white	der Weißwein(e)
with, 35	mit
woman	die Frau(en)
word, 3	das Wort(¨er)
to work, 42	arbeiten
to work (function), 9	funktionieren
World cup, 39	die Fußballwelt-meisterschaft(en)
to write, 44	schreiben
to write down, 3	aufschreiben
wrong number, 15	falsch verbunden
year, 54	das Jahr(e)
year (school), 43	die Klasse(n)
yes, 3	ja
yesterday, 54	gestern
young	jung
youth fare, 7	der Fahrpreis(e) für Jugendliche
youth hostel, 5, 10	die Jugendher-berge(n)
yuppie, 37	der Yuppie(s)*
zip, 26	der Reißverschluß(¨sse)

First published in 1990 by Usborne Publishing Ltd.
Usborne House, 83-85 Saffron Hill
London EC1N 8RT, England

Printed in Spain.